THE FRYING PAN OF DOOM

CIMORENE AND MENDANBAR settled the crowns on their heads just as Willin came through the doorway with a young man carrying a large cast-iron frying pan.

"Your Majesties, Tamriff of High Holes wishes an audience."

"Thank you, Willin," said the King. "What did you want to see us about, Tamriff?"

"This," Tamriff replied, carefully raising the frying pan.

"What does it do?" Cimorene asked. "Make gourmet meals, or just instant eggs-and-bacon for however many people you need to feed?"

The young man sighed. "No. That's the problem. It's a weapon."

"A weapon? It's a *frying pan*."

"My father is an enchanter," Tamriff explained. "He decided to create the ultimate weapon, something powerful and wondrous that heroes would fight over for centuries. The Sword of Doom he wanted to call it. Only Mother came in with the frying pan at just the wrong minute and the spell went wrong and fixed itself to the frying pan."

Mendanbar blinked. "The Frying Pan of Doom. How . . . unusual."

—From the Enchanted Forest story, "Utensile Strength"

BOOK OF
ENCHANTMENTS

BOOK OF ENCHANTMENTS

Patricia C. Wrede

Magic Carpet Books
Harcourt, Inc.

Orlando   Austin   New York   San Diego   Toronto   London

www.HarcourtBooks.com

First Magic Carpet Books edition 2005
Magic Carpet Books is a trademark of Harcourt, Inc., registered in the
United States of America and/or other jurisdictions.

The Library of Congress has cataloged the hardcover edition as follows:
Wrede, Patricia C., 1953–
Book of enchantments/Patricia C. Wrede.
p. cm.
Contents: Rikki and the wizard—The Princess, the cat, and the unicorn—Roses
by moonlight—The sixty-two curses of Caliph Arenschadd—Earthwitch—The
sword-seller—The Lorelei—Stronger than time—Cruel sisters—Utensile
strength.
1. Magic—Juvenile fiction.   2. Children's stories, American
[1. Magic—Fiction.   2. Short stories.]   I. Title.
PZ7.W91Bo 1996
[Fic]—dc20   94-41036
ISBN 0-15-201255-9
ISBN 0-15-205508-8 pb

Text set in Perpetua
Designed by Lydia D'moch

A C E G H F D B

Printed in the United States of America

Permissions Acknowledgments begin on page 235
and constitute a continuation of the copyright page

For the people who urged me
to try writing short:
Jane Yolen and the denizens
of Fidonet WRITING echo

CONTENTS

BOOK OF
ENCHANTMENTS

Rikiki and the Wizard

A S'Rian Folk Story

ONCE THERE WAS A WIZARD whose luck time was three days long. He was the luckiest wizard in the world, and he worked hard at his magic. He did a good business working spells for the people of Liavek. But the wizard was not satisfied.

He bought himself musty dusty books in Old Tichenese and burned sheep-fat lamps until late at night while he read them and practiced the spells they contained. Soon he had a house on Wizards' Row, and the Levar himself was buying spells from him. But the wizard was not satisfied.

He traveled to faraway places to learn their magics, then went into his cellar and invented spells of his own. He became the best wizard in the world, as well as the luckiest. People came from Ka Zhir and Tichen and even from the Farlands just to buy spells from him. The wizard became very rich and very famous. But he was still not satisfied.

"Everyone knows who I am now," he said to himself. "But in a few hundred years they will not remember me. I must find a way to make my reputation last."

Now, the wizard had a daughter of whom he was very proud. She had skin like a flower petal, and long hair that fell down to her feet, and bright black eyes that danced like the sun on the Sea of Luck. She was the most beautiful woman in seven cities, and her name was Ryvenna.

The wizard decided to call on the gods and offer his daughter in marriage to whichever one would promise to make him so rich and so famous that he would never be forgotten for as long as people lived around the Sea of Luck. "For," he thought, "not only will I be as rich and famous as anyone could desire, I will also get my Ryvenna a husband worthy of her beauty."

The wizard made his preparations and cast his spells. He worked for a week to get everything right. But the gods were angry with him, because he had never asked his daughter whether she agreed to his plan.

"Bad enough that he presumes we'd want her,"

grumbled Welenen the Rain-Bringer. "But giving the girl away without telling her? He acts as if she were a pet dog or a camel!" And the other gods agreed.

So when the wizard cast his spell, none of the gods would answer. He called and called, for two days and for three days, and nothing happened. Finally he resolved to try one last time. He set out the gold wire and burned the last of the special herbs and put all of his luck into the spell (and he was the luckiest wizard in the world).

Now, Rikiki had been at the meeting where all the gods agreed not to answer the wizard's summons, and he had agreed with them. But Rikiki is a blue chipmunk, and chipmunks do not have long memories. Furthermore, they are insatiably curious. When the wizard put all his effort into his last try, Rikiki couldn't resist answering, just to see what was happening. So when the smoke cleared, the wizard saw a blue chipmunk sitting before him, looking up at him with black eyes. "Nuts?" asked Rikiki.

The wizard was very angry to find that the only god who had answered his summons was a blue chipmunk. But Rikiki *was* a god, so the wizard said, "Rikiki! I will give you my daughter, who is the most beautiful woman in seven cities, if you will make me as rich and famous as I desire!"

"Daughter?" said Rikiki. "What daughter? New kind of nut?"

"No! She is a woman, the most beautiful woman

in seven cities, and I will give her to you if you do as I ask!"

"Oh!" said Rikiki. "Seven cities of nuts! What want?"

"No, no! My daughter, not nuts!"

"Daughter? Don't want daughter. Want nuts! Where nuts?"

By this time, the wizard had decided that Rikiki was no use to him, so he said, "North, Rikiki. North along the shore of the Sea of Luck. Lots of nuts, Rikiki!"

"Good!" said Rikiki. "Like nuts!" And he scurried out of the wizard's house and ran north. He ran up and down the shore of the Sea of Luck, looking for the nuts the wizard had promised, but he didn't find any. He dug holes in the ground, looking for the nuts. The dirt that he threw out of the holes became the Silverspine Mountains, but Rikiki didn't find any nuts. So he went back to the wizard's house.

"No nuts north!" said Rikiki. "Where nuts?"

"I don't have any nuts!" said the wizard. "Go away!"

"Said nuts north. Didn't find nuts. Want nuts! Where look?"

"Go west, Rikiki," said the wizard. "Go a long, long way. Find nuts. And don't come back!"

"Good!" said Rikiki. "Like nuts!" And he scurried out of the wizard's house and ran west. He ran for a long, long time, but he didn't find any nuts.

Finally he came to a mountain range on the other side of the plains. "No nuts here," said Rikiki, and he turned around and went back. It was midday and the sun was very hot. Rikiki let his tail droop on the ground as he ran, and it made a line in the dusty ground. The line became the Cat River. But Rikiki still didn't find any nuts. So he went to see the wizard again.

"No nuts west!" Rikiki said when he got back to the wizard's house. "Where nuts?"

"Not again!" said the wizard.

"Want nuts!" Rikiki insisted. He looked at the wizard with his black eyes.

The wizard remembered that Rikiki was a god, and he began to be a little frightened. "No nuts here, Rikiki," he said.

"Promised nuts!" said Rikiki. "Where?"

The wizard thought for a moment, then he said, "Go south, Rikiki. Go a long, long way south." He knew that south of Liavek is the Sea of Luck, and he was sure that it was deep enough and wide enough to drown a chipmunk, even if the chipmunk was a god.

Rikiki nodded and scurried off. The wizard heaved a sigh of relief and sat down to think of some other way to become rich and famous forever.

Now, the wizard's daughter Ryvenna had been listening at the door since her father started his spell casting. She had thought Rikiki sounded nice, so she ran out to the Two-Copper Bazaar and bought some chestnuts from a street vendor. She returned just in

5

time to hear the wizard send Rikiki south to drown in the Sea of Luck.

Quickly, Ryvenna opened up the bag of chestnuts. When Rikiki came scurrying out, she said, "Nuts, Rikiki! Here are nuts!" and held out the bag.

Rikiki stopped. "Nuts? Nuts for Rikiki?" He came over and sat in Ryvenna's lap while she fed him all the chestnuts she had brought from the Two-Copper Bazaar. When he finished, he looked up and said hopefully, "Nice nut lady! More nuts?"

"I'm sorry, Rikiki," said Ryvenna. "They're all gone."

"Oh! Fix easy," said Rikiki. He looked at the empty bag and crossed his eyes, and the bag was full again. "More nuts!" he said, and Ryvenna fed him again.

Rikiki was finishing the second bag of nuts when the wizard came out of his study. "What is he doing here?" the wizard demanded when he saw Rikiki.

"Eating nuts," said his daughter coolly. She was annoyed with him for trying to marry her to a god without asking her, and for trying to drown Rikiki. "He made the bag fill up again after it was empty."

"I don't care about nuts!" said the wizard.

Rikiki looked up. "Not like nuts?"

"Nuts aren't worth anything for people! I want gold! I want to be famous! And I want that blue chipmunk out of my house!"

"Oh!" said Rikiki. He looked cross-eyed at the bag again, then said to Ryvenna, "Dump over."

Ryvenna turned the bag upside down. A stream of gold chestnuts fell out, more chestnuts than the bag could possibly hold. They rolled all over the floor. The wizard stood staring with his mouth open.

"Gold nuts for nice nut lady!" said Rikiki happily.

The wizard closed his mouth and swallowed twice. Then he said, "What about my fame?"

"Fame?" said Rikiki. "What fame? Fame good to eat? Like nuts?"

"No, Rikiki," Ryvenna said. "Fame is having everyone know who you are. Father wants to be so famous no one will ever forget him."

"Oh!" Rikiki thought for a minute. "Not forget?"

"That's right!" said the wizard eagerly.

Rikiki sat very still, staring at the wizard, and his tail twitched. Then he said, "Not forget! All fixed."

"You have?" said the wizard, who was beginning to regret sending Rikiki to drown in the Sea of Luck.

"All done," Rikiki replied. He looked at Ryvenna. "Nuts all gone. 'Bye, nice nut lady!" And he disappeared.

"Well," said the wizard, "there's the last of my wishes; that blasted blue chipmunk is gone."

"I thought he was cute," said Ryvenna.

"Bah! He's a silly blue god who'll do anything for nuts. It was very clever of you to get some for him. Now help me pick up these gold chestnuts he made for me; we wouldn't want to lose one."

The wizard bent over and tried to pick up one of

the golden chestnuts, but as soon as he touched it, it turned into a real chestnut. He threw it down and tried another, but the same thing happened. Only Ryvenna could pick up the golden chestnuts without changing them back into real ones, and the magic chestnut bag would only make more gold for her. Worse yet, the wizard discovered that whenever he touched one of his gold levars it, too, turned into a chestnut. So did his jeweled belts and bracelets. Even the food he ate turned into chestnuts as soon as he touched it.

The wizard tried to keep his affliction a secret, but it was impossible. Soon everyone was talking about what Rikiki had done to the luckiest wizard in the world. Even people who never bought spells and who had no dealings with magicians heard the story and laughed at it. So the wizard became more famous than ever, more famous, indeed, than he wanted to be. And his fame has lasted to this day, for people still tell his story.

Ryvenna was a clever woman, and she knew that magic does not last. The magic chestnut bag ran out in a year and a day, but before it did she had poured a goodly supply of gold chestnuts from it. She became a wealthy woman, and eventually fell in love with and married a sea captain who was as kind as he was handsome. And she never forgot to leave a bowl of nuts at the door for Rikiki every night as long as she lived.

THE PRINCESS, THE CAT, AND THE UNICORN

PRINCESS ELYSSA AND HER SISTERS lived in the tiny, comfortable kingdom of Oslett, where nothing ever seemed to go quite the way it was supposed to. The castle garden grew splendid dandelions, but refused to produce either columbine or deadly nightshade. The magic carpet had a bad case of moths and the King's prized seven-league boots only went five-and-a-half leagues at a step (six leagues, with a good tailwind).

There were, of course, compensations. None of the fairies lived close enough to come to the Princesses' christenings (though they were all most carefully invited) so there were no evil enchantments laid on any of the three Princesses. The King's second wife was neither a wicked witch nor an ogress, but a plump, motherly woman who was very fond of her stepdaughters. And the only giant in the neighborhood was a kind and elderly Frost Giant who was always invited to the castle during the hottest part of the summer (his presence cooled things off wonderfully, and he rather liked being useful).

The King's councillors, however, complained bitterly about the situation. They felt it was beneath their dignity to run a kingdom where nothing ever behaved quite as it should. They grumbled about the moths and dandelions, muttered about the five-and-a-half-league boots, and remonstrated with the Queen and the three Princesses about their duties.

Elyssa was the middle Princess, and as far as the King's councillors were concerned she was the most unsatisfactory of all. Her hair was not black, like her elder sister Orand's, nor a golden corn color, like her younger sister Dacia's. Elyssa's hair was mouse brown. Her eyes were brown, too, and her chin was the sort usually described as "determined." She was also rather short, and she had a distressing tendency to freckle.

"It's all very well for a middle Princess to be ordinary," the chief of the King's councillors told her in exasperation. "But this is going too far!"

"It was only the second-best teapot," said Elyssa, who had just broken it. "And I did say I was sorry."

"If you'd only pay more attention to your duties,

things like this wouldn't happen!" the councillor huffed.

"I dusted under the throne just this morning," said Elyssa indignantly. "And it's Orand's turn to polish the crown!"

"I don't mean those duties!" the councillor snapped. "I mean the duties of your position. For instance, you and Orand ought to be fearfully jealous of Dacia, but are you? No! You won't even try."

"I should think not!" Elyssa said. "Why on earth should I be jealous of Dacia?"

"She's beautiful and accomplished and your father's favorite, and—and elder Princesses are *supposed* to dislike their younger sisters," the councillor said.

"No one could dislike Dacia," Elyssa said. "And besides, Papa wouldn't like it."

The councillor sighed, for this was undoubtedly true. "Couldn't you and Orand steal a magic ring from her?" he pleaded. "Just for form's sake?"

"Absolutely not," Elyssa said firmly, and left to get a broom to sweep up the remains of the teapot.

But the councillors refused to give up. They badgered and pestered and hounded poor Elyssa until she simply could not bear it anymore. Finally she went to her stepmother, the Queen, and complained.

"Hmmph," said the Queen. "They're being ridiculous, as usual. I could have your father talk to them, if you wish."

"It won't do any good," Elyssa said.

"You're probably right," the Queen agreed, and they sat for a moment in gloomy silence.

"I wish I could just run off to seek my fortune," Elyssa said with a sigh.

Her stepmother straightened up suddenly. "Of course! The very thing. Why didn't I think of that?"

"But I'm the *middle* Princess," Elyssa said. "It's youngest Princesses who go off to seek their fortunes."

"You've been listening to those councillors too much," the Queen said. "They won't like it, of course, but that will be good for them." The Queen was not at all fond of the councillors because they kept trying to persuade her to turn her stepdaughters into swans or throw them out of the castle while the King was away.

"It would be fun to try," Elyssa said in a wistful tone. She had always liked the idea of running off to seek her fortune, even if most of the stories did make it sound rather uncomfortable.

"It's the perfect solution," the Queen assured her. "I'll arrange with your father to leave the East Gate unlocked tomorrow night, so you can get out. Orand and Dacia can help you pack. And I'll write you a reference to Queen Hildegard from two kingdoms over, so you'll be able to find a nice job as a kitchen maid. We won't tell the councillors a thing until after you've left."

To Elyssa's surprise, the entire Royal Family was

positively enthusiastic about the scheme. Orand and Dacia had a long, happy argument about just what Elyssa ought to carry in her little bundle. The King kissed her cheek and told her she was a good girl and he hoped she would give the councillors one in the eye. And the Queen offered Elyssa the magic ring she had worn when *she* was a girl going off on adventures. (The ring turned out to have been swallowed by the castle cat, so Elyssa didn't get to take it with her after all. Still, as she told her stepmother, it was the thought that counted.) All in all, by the time Elyssa slipped out of the postern door and set off into the darkness, she was downright happy to be getting away.

As she tiptoed across the drawbridge, Elyssa stepped on something that gave a loud yowl. Hastily, she pulled her foot back and crouched down, hoping none of the councillors had heard. She could just make out the shape of the castle cat, staring at her with glowing, reproachful eyes.

"Shhhh," she said. "Poor puss! Shhh. It's all right."

"It is not all right," said the cat crossly. "How would you like to have your tail stepped on?"

"I don't have a tail," Elyssa said, considerably startled. "And if you hadn't been lying in front of me, I wouldn't have stepped on you."

"Cat's privilege," said the cat, and began furiously washing his injured tail.

"Well, I'm very sorry," Elyssa said. "But I really

must be going." She stood up and picked up her bundle again.

"I don't know how you expect to get anywhere when you can't see where you're going," said the cat.

"I certainly won't get anywhere if I stay here waiting for the sun to come up," Elyssa said sharply. "Or do you have some other suggestion?"

"You could carry me on your shoulder, and I could tell you which way to go," the cat replied. "*I* can see in the dark," he added smugly.

"All right," Elyssa said, and the cat jumped up on her shoulder.

"That way, Princess," the cat said, and Elyssa started walking.

"How is it you can talk?" she asked, as she picked her way carefully through the darkness according to the cat's directions. "You never did before."

"I think it was that ring of your stepmother's I swallowed yesterday," the cat said. He sounded uneasy and uncomfortable, as if he really didn't want to discuss the matter. So, having been well brought up, Elyssa changed the subject. They chatted comfortably about the castle cooks and the King's councillors as they walked, and periodically the cat would pat Elyssa's cheek with one velvet paw and tell her to turn this way or that way. Finally the cat announced that they had come far enough for one night, and they settled down to sleep in a little hollow.

When she awoke next morning, the first thing

Elyssa noticed were the trees. They were huge; the smallest branches she could see were three times the size of her waist, and she couldn't begin to reach around the trunks themselves. The ground was covered with green, spongy moss, and the little flowers growing out of it looked like faces. Elyssa glanced around for the cat. He was sitting in a patch of sunlight with his tail curled around his front paws, staring at her.

"This is the Enchanted Forest, isn't it?" she said accusingly.

"Right the first time, Princess," said the cat.

Elyssa frowned. She knew enough about the Enchanted Forest to be very uncomfortable about wandering around in it. It lay a little to the east of the kingdom of Oslett, and the castle had permanently mislaid at least two milkmaids and a woodcutter's son who had carelessly wandered too far in that direction. The Enchanted Forest was one of those places that is very easy to get into, but very hard to get out of again.

"But I was supposed to go to Queen Hildegard's!" Elyssa said at last.

"You wouldn't have liked Hildegard at all," the cat said seriously. "She's fat and bossy, and she has a bad-tempered, unattractive daughter to provide for. She'd be worse than the King's chief councillor, in fact."

"I don't believe you," Elyssa said. "Stepmama wouldn't send me to a person like that."

"Your stepmother hasn't seen Queen Hildegard since they were at school together twenty-some years ago," said the cat. "You're much better off here. Believe me, I know."

Elyssa was very annoyed, but it was much too late to do anything about the situation. So she picked up her bundle and set off in search of something to eat, leaving the cat to wash his back. After a little while, Elyssa found a bush with dark green leaves and bright purple berries. The berries looked very good, despite their unusual color, and she leaned forward to pick a few for breakfast.

"Don't do that, Princess," said the cat.

"Where did you come from?" Elyssa demanded crossly.

"I followed you," the cat answered. "And I wouldn't eat any of those berries, if I were you. They'll turn you into a rabbit."

Elyssa hastily dropped the berry she was holding and wiped her hand on her skirt. "Thank you for warning me," she said. "I don't suppose you know of anything around here that I *can* eat? Or at least drink? I'm very thirsty."

"As a matter of fact, there's a pool over this way," said the cat. "Follow me."

The cat led her through the trees in a winding route that Elyssa was sure would bring them right back to where they had started. She was about to say as much when she came around the bole of a tree into a moss-lined hollow. Green light filtered through the canopy of leaves onto the dark moss. In the center of the hollow, a ring of star-shaped white flowers surrounded a still, silent, mirror-dark pool of crystal-clear water.

"How lovely!" Elyssa whispered.

"I thought you were thirsty," said the cat. His tail twitched nervously as he spoke.

"I am," Elyssa said. "But— Oh, never mind." She knelt down beside the pool and scooped up a little of the water in her cupped hands.

"Who steals the water from the unicorn's pool?" demanded a voice like chiming bells.

Elyssa started, spilling the water down the front of her dress. "Drat!" she said. "Now look what you've made me do!"

As she spoke, she looked up, expecting to see the person who had spoken. There was no one there, but the chiming voice spoke again, in stern accents. "Who steals the water from the unicorn's pool?"

Elyssa wiped her hands on the dry portion of her skirt and cast a reproachful look at the cat. "I am Elyssa, Princess of Oslett, and I'm very thirsty," she said in her best royal voice. "So if you don't mind—"

"A Princess?" said the chiming voice. "Really! Well, it's about time. Let me get a look at you."

A breath of air, scented with violets and cinnamon, touched Elyssa's face. An instant later, a unicorn stepped delicately out of the woods. It halted on the other side of the pool and stood poised, its head raised to display the sharp, shining ivory horn, its mane flowing in perfect waves along its neck. Its eyes shone like sapphires, and its coat made Elyssa think of the white silk her stepmother was saving for Dacia's wedding dress.

"Gracious!" Elyssa said.

"Yes, I am, aren't I?" said the unicorn complacently. It lowered its head slightly and studied Elyssa. An expression very like dismay came into its sapphire eyes. "*You're* a Princess? Are you quite sure?"

"Of course I'm sure," Elyssa replied, nettled. "I'm the second daughter of King Callwil of Oslett; ask anybody. Ask him." She waved at the cat.

The unicorn scowled. "I should hope I would never need to ask a cat for anything," it said loftily.

"Overgrown, stuck-up goat," muttered the cat.

"What did you say?" demanded the unicorn.

"Nothing that would interest you," said the cat.

"You may go, then," the unicorn said grandly.

"I'm quite happy right here," the cat said. "Or I was until you came stomping in with your silly questions."

"How dare— Princess Elyssa! What are you doing?" said the unicorn.

Elyssa took a last gulp of water and let the rest dribble through her fingers and back into the pool. "Having a drink," she said. She really *had* been very thirsty, and she had taken advantage of the argument between the cat and the unicorn to scoop up another handful of water.

"Well, I suppose it's all right, since you're a Princess," the unicorn said. Its chiming voice sounded positively sulky.

"Thank you," said Elyssa. She stood up and shook droplets from her fingers. "It's very good water."

"Of course it's good water!" the unicorn said. "A unicorn's pool is always pure and sweet and crystal clear and—"

"Yes, yes," said the cat. "But it's time we were going. Princess Elyssa has to seek her fortune, you know."

"Leave?" said the unicorn. It lifted its head in a regal gesture, and light flashed on the point of its horn. "Oh no, you can't leave. Not the Princess, anyway."

"What?" Elyssa said, considerably taken aback. "Why not?"

"Why, because you're a Princess and I'm a unicorn," the unicorn said.

"I don't see what that has to do with anything," Elyssa said.

"You will gather trefoils and buttercups and pinks for me, and plait them into garlands for my neck," the unicorn went on dreamily, as if Elyssa hadn't said anything at all. "I will rest my head in your lap, and you will polish my horn and comb my mane."

"Sounds like an exciting life," said the cat.

"Your mane doesn't need combing," Elyssa told the unicorn crossly. "And your horn doesn't need polishing. As for flowers, I'll be happy to have Stepmama send you some dandelions from the garden at home. But I'm not interested in staying here for goodness knows how long just to plait them into garlands."

"Nonsense," said the unicorn. "You're a Princess. All Princesses adore unicorns."

"Well, I don't," Elyssa said firmly. "And I'm not staying."

The cat lashed his tail in agreement and gave the unicorn a dark look.

"You don't have a choice," the unicorn said calmly. "You're not much of a Princess, but you're better than nothing, and I'm not letting you go. I've been stuck out here on the far edge of the Enchanted Forest for years and years, with no one to sing songs about me or appreciate my beauty, and I deserve some consideration."

"Not from me, you don't," Elyssa muttered. She decided that the cat had been right to call the unicorn a stuck-up goat. "I'm sorry, but we really must leave," she said in a louder tone. "Good-bye, unicorn." She picked up her bundle and started for the edge of the hollow.

The unicorn watched with glittering eyes, but it made no move to stop her. "I don't like this," the cat said as he and Elyssa left the hollow.

"You're the one who found that pool in the first place," Elyssa pointed out.

The cat ducked its head. "I know," he said uncomfortably. "But——"

He broke off abruptly as they came around one of the huge trees and found themselves at the edge of the hollow once more. The unicorn was watching them with a smug, sardonic expression from the other side of the pool.

"We must have gotten turned around in the woods," Elyssa said doubtfully.

The cat did not reply. They turned and started into the woods again. This time they walked very slowly, to be certain they did not go in a circle. In a few minutes, they were back at the hollow.

"Had enough?" said the unicorn.

"Third time lucky," said the cat. "Come on, Princess."

They turned their backs on the unicorn and walked into the woods. Elyssa concentrated very hard and kept a careful eye on the trees.

"I think we're going to make it this time," she said after a little. "Cat? Cat, where are— Oh, dear." She was standing at the edge of the hollow, looking across the pool at the unicorn.

"The cat is gone for good," the unicorn informed her in a satisfied tone.

Elyssa felt a pang of worry about her friend. "What did you do to him?" she demanded.

"I got rid of him," the unicorn said. "I don't want a cat; I want a Princess. Someone to comb my mane, and polish my horn—"

"—and make you garlands, I know," Elyssa said. "Well, I won't do it."

"No?" said the unicorn.

"No," Elyssa said firmly. "So you might as well just let me go."

"I don't think so," the unicorn said. "You'll change your mind after a while, you'll see. I'm much too beautiful to resist. And I expect that with a little work you'll improve a great deal."

"Elyssa doesn't need your kind of improvement," said the cat's voice from just above Elyssa's head.

Elyssa looked up. The cat was perched in the lowest fork of the enormous tree beside her. "You came back!" she said.

"Did you really think I wouldn't, Princess?" said the cat. "I'd have gotten here sooner, but I wanted to make sure of the way out. Just in case you've had enough of our conceited friend."

"You're bluffing, cat," said the unicorn. "Princess Elyssa can't get out unless I let her, and I won't."

"That's what you think," said the cat. "Shall we go, Princess?"

"Yes, *please*," said Elyssa.

"Put your hand on my back, then, and don't let go," said the cat.

Elyssa bent over and put her hand on the cat's

back, just below his neck. It was a very awkward and uncomfortable way to walk, and she was sure she looked quite silly. She had to concentrate very hard to keep from falling or tripping and losing her hold as she sidled along. "How much farther?" she asked after what seemed a long time.

"Not far," said the cat. Elyssa thought he sounded tired. A few moments later they entered a large clearing (which contained neither a pool nor a unicorn), and the cat stopped. "All right, Princess," the cat said. "You can let go now."

Elyssa took her hand off the cat's back and straightened up. It felt very good to stretch again. When she looked down, the cat was lowering himself to the ground in a stiff and clumsy fashion that was quite unlike his usual grace.

"Oh, dear," said Elyssa. She dropped to her knees beside the cat and stroked his fur, very gently. "Are you all right, cat?" she asked, because she couldn't think of anything else to say.

The cat did not answer. Elyssa remembered all the stories she had ever heard about animals who had been gravely injured or even killed getting their masters or mistresses out of trouble, and she began to be very much afraid. "Please be all right, cat," she said, and leaned over and kissed him on the nose.

The air shimmered, and then it rippled, and then it exploded into brightness right in front of Elyssa's eyes. She blinked. An exceedingly handsome man dressed in brown velvet lay sprawled on the moss in front of her, right where the cat had been.

Elyssa blinked again. The man propped his head on one elbow and looked up at her. "Very nice, Princess," he said. "But I wouldn't mind if you tried again a little lower down."

"You're the cat, aren't you?" Elyssa said.

"I was," the man admitted. He sat up and smiled at her. "You don't object to the change, do you?"

"No," said Elyssa. "But who are you now, please?"

"Prince Riddle of Amonhill," the man said. He bowed to her even though he was still sitting down, which proved he was a Prince. "I made the mistake of stopping at Queen Hildegard's castle some time ago, and she changed me into a cat when I refused to marry her dreadful daughter."

"Queen Hildegard? But I was supposed to go see her!" Elyssa exclaimed.

"I know. I told you you wouldn't like her," Prince Riddle said. "She condemned me to be a cat until I was kissed by a Princess who had drunk the water from a unicorn's pool. Her daughter was the only Princess the Queen knew of who had tasted the water. If she had also managed to kiss me I'd have had to marry her." He shuddered.

"I see," said Elyssa slowly. "So that's why you brought me to the Enchanted Forest and then found the unicorn's pool."

Riddle looked a little shamefaced. "Yes. I didn't expect to have any trouble with the unicorn; they usually aren't around much. I'm sorry."

"It's quite all right," Elyssa said hastily. "It was very interesting. And I'm glad I could help you. And—and you don't need to think that you have to marry me just because I disenchanted you."

"It *is* traditional, you know," Riddle said, with a sidelong glance that reminded Elyssa very strongly of the cat.

"Well, I think it's a silly tradition!" Elyssa said in an emphatic tone. "What if you didn't like the Princess who broke the spell?"

Riddle smiled warmly. "But I do like you, Princess."

"Oh," said Elyssa.

"You were always very nice to me when I was a cat."

"Yes," said Elyssa.

"And I like the idea of marrying you." Riddle looked at her a little uncertainly. "That is, if you wouldn't mind marrying me."

"Actually," said Elyssa, "I'd like it very much."

So Elyssa and Riddle went back to the castle to be married. Elyssa's family was delighted. Her papa kissed her cheek and clapped Riddle on the back. Her stepmama cried with joy and then was happily scandalized to hear about the doings of her old school friend Queen Hildegard. And both of Elyssa's sisters agreed to be bridesmaids (much to the dismay of the King's councillors, who felt that it was bad enough for a middle Princess to be married first without emphasizing the fact by having her sisters stand up for her).

The wedding was a grand affair, with all the neighboring Kings and Queens in attendance. There were even a couple of fairies present, which made the King's councillors more cross than ever. (Fairies, according to the chief councillor, were supposed to come to christenings, not to weddings.) After the wedding, Elyssa had her stepmama send a special note to Queen Hildegard. A few days later, Queen Hildegard's daughter disappeared into the Enchanted Forest, and shortly thereafter rumors began circulating that the unicorn had found a handmaiden even more conceited than it was.

And so they all lived happily for the rest of their lives, except the King's councillors, who never would stop trying to make things go the way they thought things ought to be.

ROSES BY MOONLIGHT

LIGHT AND THE RAUCOUS NOISE of a heavy-metal band spilled from the long, open windows onto the patio outside, overwhelming the pale reflected gleam of the full moon and drowning the hum of the cicadas. Even from halfway down the long drive, where she leaned against the hood of her mother's Lexus, Adrian could feel the bass beat thumping in her bones. Samantha's music, Samantha's friends, Samantha's party. It was a good thing they had no near neighbors to complain. Not that anyone would have. No one but Adrian ever complained about the outrageous things her younger sister did.

I don't mind Dad throwing her a party, Adrian told

herself for the hundredth time. *Really, I don't. But the way she swept in, like the prodigal daughter coming home . . . yes, I mind that. And—— Oh, I don't know. Why can't things be simple?*

She looked down at the half-inch worm of ash on the end of her cigarette and grimaced. *My only vice, and I don't even enjoy it.* Still, it was a good excuse to avoid the party; most of Sam's friends were into clean air and health food. She dropped the cigarette and ground the tip into the cement, then tilted her head back to stare at the sky. The moon hung overhead like an old dime worn smooth and shiny. *Almost midnight. I wonder how much longer they'll go on. Dawn, probably. Can I spend another five hours smoking? I don't think I have that many cigarettes.*

The music trailed off in a series of erratic crashes. After a moment's blessed silence, it began again, loud and indecipherable even at this distance. Adrian sighed and pushed away from the Lexus. Maybe if she walked farther down the drive the noise wouldn't bother her so much.

"Adrian."

Startled, she turned. "Hello, Mother. Did Dad send you——" *—to get me to put in a token appearance at his favorite daughter's home-from-prep-school bash?* "—to talk to me?"

"No." Her mother's voice was quiet and level, as always; Adrian almost lost the reply in a rattle of drumbeats.

"I came out to smoke." The words sounded sullen even to her own ears. Defiantly, she fumbled for a cigarette. She almost dropped it twice before she got it lit.

"Of course, dear."

Adrian looked sharply across the hood of the car. Her mother's expression—or at least as much of it as Adrian could distinguish in the dim light—was as polite and nonjudgmental as her voice had been. But she was always polite and nonjudgmental.

The drums erupted again, with the wail of a highly augmented electric guitar as counterpoint. When the sound subsided to a more normal level, Adrian's mother said mildly, "It's a bit noisy, isn't it? Adrian . . ."

She's going to ask me to go back in and pretend I'm as glad to see Sam as everyone else is. I'd rather stay here and pretend to chain-smoke. "What?"

"I'm afraid I haven't done as well for you as I ought."

Speechless, Adrian stared. Darkness and moon shadows combined with her mother's habitual reserve to make her expression unreadable. After a moment, the calm voice continued, "It's late to be thinking of this, I know. But when you go off to college next fall, I'd like to think . . ." She paused, looking up at the house.

Not knowing what to say, Adrian took a long pull on her cigarette. As she blew a thin stream of smoke that frayed quickly into nothingness, her mother began to speak again.

"I grew up poor, Adrian. Dirt poor. My father ran off when I was four and never came back. Sometimes I think I can just remember him. Mama had nothing but three babies to raise. This"—she made a sweeping gesture that took in the manicured grounds, the graceful curve of the driveway, the Lexus, the house, and somehow even the heavy-metal band and the party inside—"this was my dream, then. Money, lots of money, and a man who wouldn't leave me and his children, no matter what."

Adrian shifted uneasily. She'd heard the story many times; her mother had never made a secret of her background. But this time there was a hard edge to the tale that she'd never noticed before. "Mother, what are you trying to—"

"Tonight is a sort of anniversary for me," her mother went on without seeming to hear. "On this night, twenty-one years ago, I started on my way to all this."

"I thought you met Dad in September."

"Oh, that . . . Yes. I did. September first, twenty-one years ago this fall." She smiled in the moonlight; then the smile faded. "But tonight is the real anniversary, though I've never told anyone. This was my dream, and when I had the opportunity to make it happen, I snatched it. I never looked beyond it, never thought there might be other dreams . . ."

"Mother, are you and Dad . . . I mean, aren't you happy?"

"Happy enough, dear, and it is the life I chose." She looked at Adrian. "And no, your father and I aren't contemplating a divorce, if that's what you're frowning about."

"Good." The strength of her reaction surprised her.

Her mother turned toward the house once more. "Adrian, I'd like you to do a favor for me."

"What favor?"

"Stay out here for another hour or so. There's someone I'd like you to meet, and I'm sure she'll come tonight. Almost sure. It's a seventh year. And if you are given a choice . . . be careful, be wise. Don't rush to pick one dream before you've even looked at the others."

"I don't understand."

"You will." Her mother looked at her watch. "It's five minutes to midnight. I must go in. You will stay?"

"Yes."

"Good. Good night, dear. I'll see you in the morning."

Adrian watched her mother walk up the drive to the house. *I wish I knew what that was all about. Well, at least now I have a good excuse to avoid the party.* She flicked her cigarette and watched the live sparks scatter on the summer breeze. The band stopped. A moment later, a breathless, overamplified voice said something about the end of the set; in another few seconds, Sam and her friends would be piling out onto the patio. Adrian flicked her cigarette again, for the pleasure of watching the sparks, then dropped it, stepped on the tip to put it out, and walked toward the back of the Lexus. No sense in making it easy for them to spot her. Suddenly, she stopped.

Behind the car stood a woman. She looked very little older than Adrian and she was tall and slim as a model. Her hair was dark—chestnut, probably, though in the moonlight it looked black—unfashionably long and straight, with a silver sheen of moonlight across it like a veil. Her face and features were almost classic, saved from a boring perfection by a chin that was a trifle too pointed and dark eyes a hair too widely set. She wore a silk dress whose flowing and deceptively simple lines proclaimed it the work of an expensive designer.

"You are Adrian, the eldest daughter of this house." The woman's voice was quiet and full of music, and Adrian was instantly certain that she was not one of Sam's crowd. In thirty years, one or two of them might learn such self-possession, but none of them had it now.

Adrian felt a stab of envy. Quashing it firmly, she answered, "Yes. You must be Mother's friend."

"Your mother spoke of me?"

"She only said that she hoped you'd come tonight

and that she wanted me to meet you." Adrian hesitated, but something made her add, "And that I should be careful."

"Ah." The woman smiled. "Good advice in many circumstances." She studied Adrian briefly, then nodded. "Her blood runs true in you."

"Most people say I look like my father."

"I was not speaking of your looks. Come; walk with me. I would learn more of you."

Laughter drifted down from the house as they started down the drive. Adrian glanced back and grimaced in spite of herself.

"Your sister's guests give you no pleasure," the woman said. "Do you dislike them? Or is it her involvement that disturbs you?"

"No, it's not like that at all," Adrian said. "Samantha is—Sam, that's all. She doesn't think how things are for other people. She just does what she wants, and it always works. She's . . . she's like the youngest child in a fairy tale, the one who goes off on a quest riding a goat and carrying ten copper pennies, and comes back with the steed of the North Wind, the apples of the sun, and the keys to six kingdoms."

"And you?"

"Oh, I'm the envious older sister, who gets pushed down a well at the end of the story." She had meant for it to sound lighthearted; it came out harsh, almost bitter. Hastily, she added, "Sam's my sister; I'm glad things go so well for her, I really am. I just wish, sometimes . . ." She couldn't bring herself to finish the sentence. *And why am I telling her all this, anyway?*

"I see. But you are too wise to take her walking on the cold sea strand."

"Sam's hair is too short to string a harp. Anyway, the way her life goes, the harper would pull her out long before she drowned." Adrian shrugged. "I've always known that Sam got the looks and luck in this family; I just have to make do with the brains."

The woman turned to look at Adrian and after a moment said, "You do yourself injustice as to beauty. As for fortune, that may change, if it has not already."

"You sound like my mother. Not that I don't appreciate the kind words."

The woman laughed, a silvery, musical sound. "You are courteous indeed. It has been long and long since any named me kind." She studied Adrian again, then half nodded to herself. "Such courtesy deserves reward. Come walk with me among the roses, and let what may be, be."

"Roses?" Adrian stopped. "I'm afraid there aren't any. Mother says they're too much trouble."

"Does she."

"Well, they have to be sprayed all the time or they get black spot or mildew or something. And they need a lot of pruning, and it's a nuisance. So Mother won't have any in the gardens."

"Your mother has more humor in her than I thought. Yet follow me, and you shall see my meaning."

Without waiting to see whether Adrian would comply, the woman moved on ahead. Automatically, Adrian started after her, then stopped. *If she wants to go on a wild goose chase over half the grounds—*

The distant thump of the drums began again. *The set break is over already? Sam must have really charmed the band.* Adrian looked at the rapidly moving figure ahead, then plunged after her strange companion. *Anything* was better than another two hours of sitting on the Lexus and listening to Sam's friends enjoying Sam's kind of music.

The woman moved rapidly, but with deceptive smoothness. Adrian found herself moving in an awkward compromise between running and walking, always a stumbling step or two behind. *She acts as if she knows where she's going, but how can she? She hasn't been here before, or she'd know that there aren't any roses.*

At a clumping birch on the south side of the house, the woman turned. With a sigh, Adrian followed her into the overgrown tangle of honeysuckle behind the tree. The drums were almost inaudible here; the bushes must be dense enough to absorb most of the sound. They were tall enough to cut off most of the moonlight, too. Adrian could barely see.

Fortunately, her companion had slowed down a little—well, even *she* must have some trouble with the branches.

The bushes seemed to go on for much too long. The clump in back of the birch was only about ten feet across; surely, they should have come out onto the lawn by now . . .

And then the woman stopped and held the last honeysuckle branch aside so Adrian could step clear. As the branch swung back behind her, Adrian halted, staring.

In front of her was a rose garden, washed with moonlight and heavy with the mingled perfume of many flowers. Hedge roses, laden with blossoms, formed a thick wall around the garden. At the single gap in the wall, just in front of Adrian, two climbing roses wove their way up the sides of an arched white support to meet in a tangled spray of flower-heavy branches at the top. Through the arch, curving pebble paths gleamed between drifts of rosebushes—tree roses, floribunda roses, miniature roses, tea roses, wild roses, every kind of rose she had ever seen or heard of, all blooming madly, impossibly, in the impossible garden.

Adrian turned. "How . . . ? Where did this come from? Who are you?"

"Ask rather of my roses," the woman said. "But know that I am not required to answer."

"This is impossible."

"So have others said before you. And you are wrong. My garden contains all possibilities, however strange."

"I don't understand."

"I think that soon you will, if you look closely."

The woman's smile made Adrian uncomfortable. She turned away, back to the roses. The flowers drew her. Adrian took a step forward, toward the arching entrance of the garden. Overhead, the full moon shone clear and bright, drenching the scene with enough light to make the colors of the roses dimly visible. Adrian reached out to touch one of the blossoms on the archway, a full-blown white rose nodding just beside her head. The woman's voice stopped her.

"You may take one rose from my garden, and one only. Take care that you do not break a stem by accident and find your choice made for you. Some flowers are more fragile than they first appear."

Adrian swallowed an irritated response. "I'll be careful," she said, and put both hands ostentatiously behind her back. Leaning forward, she breathed the rose's scent.

She sat in a small, cluttered room in an apartment high above a noisy city street—cluttered because Samantha kept her house bare and Spartan, in the city because Samantha preferred open country. She combed the gray hair she refused to color because Samantha kept hers a rich brown, and listened to the classical music Samantha hated, and wondered bitterly whether she had ever done anything in all her long life simply because she wanted to and not because Samantha would have done something else . . .

Adrian stiffened and pulled back. As she stared at the rose, the woman behind her said, "I did not think you would want that one."

Unable to think of a response, Adrian turned to the other side of the archway. The roses there were dark under the moonlight. In the day they would be a rich, deep crimson, assuming day ever came to this strange place. Adrian eyed a rose doubtfully for a moment, then bent forward and sniffed.

She stood on a porch, smiling as she watched her grandchildren play in the small front yard. The littlest one reminded her of her sister, Samantha, with her dark hair and eyes and her quicksilver grace. It was a pity Sam had died so young—

Adrian recoiled. Why was her mind playing such nasty tricks on her? Did these unexpected and astonishing flowers induce hallucinations, or was she imagining it all—the woman, the garden, and everything? She reached among the leaves to touch the thick, thorn-encrusted stem, then jerked her hand back with an exclamation of pain. Ruefully, she looked at the bead of blood forming on her fingertip. Not imagination, then.

"Higher up, you will find fewer thorns," the woman said.

Slowly, Adrian nodded. Reaching up, she found another of the crimson flowers and tugged the stem gently, gently, to be certain not to break it free unintentionally. On tiptoe, she breathed a whiff of the thick, sweet scent.

With a spray of snow crystals, she swung around the last pole and shot through the finishing gate. As she coasted to a stop, breathing hard, she heard the announcer giving her time. Not bad, *she thought,* not bad at all. I might win the whole Seniors Division, and not just the Over-70. *Her family was coming forward to congratulate her in a small, happy mob. She blinked suddenly and wondered why, after all these years, she should suddenly think of her dead sister at a moment of triumph . . .*

As carefully as she had pulled it toward her, Adrian released the flower. She settled back on her heels and realized she was holding her breath. It took an effort of will to begin breathing again. *Hallucinations,* she told herself, but she did not believe it. Whatever they were—false memories, mental pictures—they had too sharp an edge to be hallucinations. After a moment, she looked over at the dark-haired woman.

"What is the point of all this?" she demanded in a voice that started out fierce with anger and ended on an uncertain note. "Are you trying to tell me that the only way I'll be happy is if my sister dies? What have you got against Sam?"

"I care but little if she lives or dies," the woman replied calmly. "And hardly more than that for you, if truth be told. Yet I have not spoken of her."

"But the roses—"

"The possibilities my roses show are yours to see, and yours alone. What I know of them is what you tell me, no more. If they show you your sister, it is because she is in your thoughts tonight. Another time, they might show you other things."

"Oh." It sounded as impossible as everything else in this garden, which meant it was probably true. If any of it was. "I'm sorry. I didn't understand." *I still don't, not really, but I bet you won't explain even if I ask. And damn if I'm going to give you the satisfaction of asking.*

The woman inclined her head in acceptance of the apology and smiled slightly as if she knew the thought that had followed it. "Will you choose your flower?"

Possibilities . . . "I—I think I'd like to look at some of the ones farther in," Adrian said. "Before I make up my mind."

The woman smiled. "You are wise for one so young. Look all you wish, but remember: one rose, and one only, may you take with you when you leave. Some find the choice a hard one."

"No kidding," Adrian muttered as she turned away. She stepped under the arching roses and stopped at a waist-high bush covered with knots of pale flowers. *Not white,* she thought, glancing back at the archway to compare. *Really pale pink, maybe. Or yellow. I wish the moon were just a little brighter.* She eyed the bush a moment longer, then bent and inhaled.

Her footsteps echoed down the marble hall as she headed for Courtroom Five. This one was an open-and-shut case. She had two eyewitnesses to the assault, and there were no questions of admissibility of evidence. Samantha wasn't going to get her client off on a technicality this time. Adrian smiled as she pushed open the courtroom door.

Stepping back, Adrian stared at the rose. She could still feel the echo of the bitter rivalry between . . . herself? . . . and Sam. *I don't hate Sam,* she told herself. *I don't!* And her own treacherous mind whispered, *But you could.* Abruptly, she swung toward the next bush. Without pausing to look at the flower, she buried her nose in its petals.

The hospital room was quiet, except for the rhythmic sound of the machinery and her mother's soft weeping. She floated in a drugged haze. At least the pain had receded, though breathing was no easier. Her hands were numb and cold, and she couldn't feel her father's grip anymore. Not much longer. Somewhere in the fading distance, she heard Sam's tearful voice: "Oh, Mom, why didn't she quit smoking?"

She leaped back as if a bee had stung her nose and stood, shaking, on the gravel path between the roses. When her shivering stopped at last, she raised her eyes and surveyed the silver-shadowed garden. Surely, among so many roses there was *one* that held neither death nor bitterness. With grim purpose, she lowered her head and began methodically working her way along the path.

Doctor, actress, mother, executive, carpenter, psychologist, housewife, concert cellist, author, lawyer, social worker—the roses offered a hundred different lives for her consideration. Some were happy, some not; some pictured heady successes, others miserable failures. As she moved farther from the garden's entrance, the visions focused more on her work, her friends, her lovers and husbands and children, and less on her sister, but even in the happiest lives Adrian could feel an undercurrent of tension, a sense of some important thing left unresolved. Several times she hesitated, and once she started to reach for a rose stem before she caught herself and moved on.

As she searched, Adrian felt the amused gaze of the black-haired woman on her back, though she did not turn to look. *This is ridiculous,* she thought, stepping over a cluster of miniature roses with pale centers and dark edges. *They're flowers, that's all. Just really weird flowers.* She wondered suddenly why she had not, in all the visions the roses had shown her, seen Sam even once. She had seen herself talking with her mother and father, with friends she had known for years and with those she had not yet met, with lovers, husbands, children, and grandchildren, but not with her sister. That awful moment in the cancer ward was as close as she had come.

Shaking off a sudden chill, she bent toward a small bush at the rear of the rose bed. It took her a moment to find a blossom; the leaves were thick, and the flowers were hidden among them. She pricked her fingers twice trying to push the other stems far enough aside to get a good sniff of the rose. *This had better be a good one,* she thought. Finally, she cleared a space and breathed the rose's scent.

Samantha stood looking out the window. As the last of the funeral guests pulled away, she turned. "All right, Adrian. It's just us now, and I've got something to say to you."

"Go ahead."

For a moment, Sam hesitated, as if she could not remember the words or had suddenly changed her mind. Then her shoulders stiffened, and she said, "You've built a wall between us, Adrian, and I'm tired of knocking myself against it. I don't know why you have to disapprove of everything I do, but I don't have to live with it anymore now that Mom and Dad are both gone. So I won't. I'm leaving in a few hours, and I won't be back unless you ask."

"I might have known you'd pull something dramatic at a time like this," Adrian said, while the back of her mind whispered, Leaving? She can't leave. She doesn't mean it. She's my *sister.*

"I'm not making a dramatic gesture, however you choose to interpret it. I just thought I'd explain. Try to explain. If you won't hear it, at least it won't be because I didn't say it." She started toward the door, then paused with one hand on the knob. "It's your wall, Adrian. You're the one who has to do something about it, if anyone does." The door swung open, then shut, and she was gone, while Adrian's mind stuttered over things to say before settling at last into the familiar pattern of criticism and anger . . .

"No!" Adrian said, pulling back so rapidly that one of the thorns scratched her cheek. "It's not like that!"

"You need not be upset." The soft voice of the dark-haired woman made Adrian jump. "The roses show possibilities, nothing more."

"Then why are they all the same?"

The woman's eyebrows lifted. "The same? I do not think so. But there are always things in each one's life that are too late to change. You can but live with them, as you endure your height or the color of your eyes."

"I like the color of my eyes, and anyway it's not like that." Adrian kept her voice under control only with considerable effort. "I'm not like that. And I don't believe it's too late, no matter what your damned roses show."

The woman shrugged. "Then search."

Adrian stared, angry enough to strike her but a

little too afraid to actually do so. Then she turned and plunged into the roses, heedless of the scratches. Images blurred together: an empty stage; a marble-lined hallway full of elegant strangers; Sam lying in the sun beside a swimming pool; their mother shaking her head sadly; the black-haired woman watching impassively in the moonlit garden. None of them offered what she wanted. She was beginning to despair of ever finding it, when she saw a rosebush half hidden behind an arbor.

Even from a distance, it looked different from the other plants. Where they lifted their branches in graceful sprays, or twined over arbors, or stood neat and compact, this one sprawled untidily in a waist-high mass of leaves. Unlike the other rosebushes, it was not covered with flowers. Indeed, when she first saw it, Adrian thought it bore no blossoms at all. Drawing nearer, she saw tight, pointed buds here and there among the leaves.

How am I supposed to smell a flower that isn't open yet? Tentatively, she sniffed at one of the buds. Nothing happened. Adrian pressed her lips together and began hunting through the thick, prickly branches. At last she found a flower—still a bud, really, with the tips of the petals barely beginning to unfurl. She stared at it for a moment, then leaned forward.

"Do you think it's been easy for me, being your sister?" Samantha asked quietly. "Always coming second, being expected to be as brilliant and talented—"

45

"*Don't try to flatter me,*" Adrian said, but somehow the words lacked the bitterness they would have held even half an hour before. It had never occurred to her before that their relationship might have made things difficult for Sam. Sam was the one who was difficult.

"*I'm not. Don't you know that's how they all think of you? I have to be twice as much of anything just to get noticed.*"

"*Is that why . . . ?*" Adrian stopped and swallowed. "*Look, Sam, I . . . Well, I'm sorry.*" She felt as if the words had been wrenched out of her with pliers, and then she felt almost light-headed. "*Do you suppose we can do better from now on?*"

Samantha smiled suddenly. "*Maybe if we both try.*"

Adrian rocked back, staring at the bud. Was it that simple? But it hadn't seemed simple, even in the brief image. It had seemed . . . hard. Letting go of anger should be easy, now that she knew how much trouble it would make and how much of it was due to willful blindness. It should be easy, but she could tell that it wasn't going to be.

There was a whisper of movement behind her. "Have you at last unearthed a flower that suits you?" the black-haired woman asked.

"I think— Yes. Yes, I have." But Adrian's hands seemed paralyzed, frozen to the branches they were holding back. She could not move to pick the rose; she could only look.

"If you are sure, then take it."

The momentary paralysis left Adrian, and she reached for the rose. And paused. *If you are given a choice, be careful; be wise. I never thought there might be other dreams* . . . She sat in a garden of dreams, surrounded by possibilities, but to choose one, no matter how much she desired it, precluded all the others. There had been wonderful things in some of those roses. Slowly, Adrian drew her hand back.

"I think not," she said. "It's only just opened. It ought to have a chance to bloom."

The woman's eyebrows rose. "One visit to my garden is more than many mortals gain. You will not have a second chance to pick a rose."

"Then I'll make my life up as I go along, the way everybody else does." Gently, Adrian withdrew her hands, letting the leaves close over the flower. She stood and turned to look directly at the strange woman. "Thank you very much for the offer, though. It's been . . . a real education."

The woman winced; then the ghost of a smile touched her lips. "You are wiser than most of those who come to see my roses."

"That depends on how it turns out, doesn't it?" Adrian looked at the hundreds of flowers shining in the moonlight and shivered slightly.

"It does. Yet I think that all may yet be very well for you." The woman's smile grew broader. "It will interest me to watch and see."

"I think I'd better get home. Sam's having a party, and I really shouldn't miss all of it."

"You may return the way we came, down the path and between the rose arch," the woman said. "I shall not come with you, though we may meet again in after years, if you are willing."

Adrian was surprised to find herself nodding. "Good night."

"Fare you well."

Turning, Adrian walked toward the garden's entrance. As she ducked into the thicket outside, she felt the packet of cigarettes in her pocket shift. *The first thing I do is get rid of those,* she thought, remembering the hospital. *And then I'll talk to Sam.*

She came out of the honeysuckle and smiled at the familiar birches. The band was thumping loudly, building to some sort of climax. It all but drowned out the crackle of the cellophane cigarette wrapper in her pocket. *There's half a pack left. It'd be a shame to waste them. And I still don't want to go to the party.*

Adrian looked at the house once more, then headed back the way she had come, toward the parked cars.

Tomorrow, I'll throw the rest of them away, if there are any left. Tomorrow, I'll talk to Sam.

Tomorrow.

THE SIXTY-TWO CURSES OF CALIPH ARENSCHADD

THE WORST THING about Caliph Arenschadd is that he's a wizard. At least that's what my father says. Mother says the worst thing about the caliph is his temper, and that it's a good thing he's a wizard because if he were just an ordinary caliph he'd cut people's heads off when they displeased him, instead of cursing them.

I tend to agree with Mother. Cutting someone's head off is permanent; a curse, you can break. Of course, it usually takes something nasty and undignified to do it, but everything about curses is supposed to be unpleasant. Father doesn't see it that way. I think he'd prefer to be permanently dead than temporarily undignified.

Father is Caliph Arenschadd's grand vizier, which is the reason all of us have opinions about the caliph and his curses. You see, a long time ago the caliph decided that he would lay a curse on anyone who displeased him, thus punishing the person and displaying the caliph's magical skill at the same time. (Mother also says Caliph Arenschadd likes to show off.) He found out very quickly that it was hard work coming up with a new curse every time someone made him unhappy, but by then he'd had a proclamation issued and he couldn't back down. So he shut himself up in one of the palace minarets for weeks, and when he came out he had a list of sixty-two curses he could cast at a moment's notice.

From then on, every time someone has done something the caliph doesn't like, the caliph has hauled out his list of curses and slapped one on whoever-it-was. Everyone starts at the first curse on the list and works their way down, so you can tell how long someone's been at court by whether his fingernails are three feet long or his eyelids stuck together. Father's been at court longer than anybody, so we've worked our way through an awful lot of curses.

I say *we* because Caliph Arenschadd doesn't just curse the particular person he's annoyed with. His curses get the person's whole family as well. I don't think that's fair, but Mother says it's just like him.

She's been mad at the caliph ever since the eleventh curse, which made all three of us lose our voices for a week right in the middle of the Enchantresses and Sorceresses Annual Conference. Mother was supposed to present a paper, but she had to cancel it because she couldn't talk, and she's never forgiven Caliph Arenschadd.

I have to admit that some of the curses are fun. I enjoyed being bright green, and having monkey's paws was quite useful (I like climbing things, and the peaches had just turned ripe). Having my eyelids stuck together was boring, though. Things even out. It's best when you know what to expect, but after Father passed the forty-second curse there wasn't anyone ahead of us anymore to let us know what came next. We muddled through curses number forty-three through forty-seven with only a little more trouble than usual, and Caliph Arenschadd actually seemed pleased. We went for almost three months without any curses at all. Then one day Father came home from the palace looking grim and solemn.

Mother took one look at him and said, "O my husband and light of my eyes, not *again!*" in the exasperated tone she usually saves for me when I've put a rip in my skirts.

"I'm afraid so, Mirza," Father said. "He was in an awful mood today, but I simply couldn't put off asking him about those water rights for the caravaners any longer. So we're going to find out about number forty-eight." Father never says the word *curse* when he's talking about one of Caliph Arenschadd's; he only refers to them by number.

"Someone should take that caliph in hand," Mother said.

"Are you offering?" Father demanded.

I could tell there was an argument starting, so I got up and slipped out of the room before they could get me in on it. Mother and Father usually have an argument right after Caliph Arenschadd puts another curse on us; I think it relieves their feelings or something. It never lasts long, and as soon as they're finished they start looking for the way to break the curse. They're very good at it. Most of the curses last less than a week, and the longest one only went nine days. It's never much fun to be around for the arguing part, though, which is why I left.

I went to visit my best friend, Tumpkin. Tumpkin isn't his real name; I call him that because the first time I met him he wouldn't tell me who he was and I had to call him something. I ran into him in one of the private gardens at the palace, so I figured he was one of the caliph's pages, poking around where he wasn't supposed to be. He's about the same age as I am, and he's nearsighted and sort of pudgy—just the kind of kid that gets picked on all the time. That's why I started calling him Tumpkin; it seemed to fit.

I didn't have to spend much time looking for Tumpkin on the first day of the forty-eighth curse. He was in his favorite spot, under a bush behind a gold garden seat. He heard me coming and looked up. When he saw who it was, he grinned at me in relief. "Imani!" he said. "I was just thinking about you."

"You ought to be thinking about your duties," I told him. "Someone's going to catch you shirking one of these days, and then you'll really be in trouble."

"Do *you* have to tell me what to do, too?" Tumpkin said grumpily. He waved in the direction of the palace. "You sound just like everyone in there."

"No, I sound like my father," I said, flopping down on the bench. "Sorry, it's been a rough day."

Tumpkin stopped looking grumpy and looked interested and sympathetic instead. "What happened?"

"Father picked up another curse, and he and Mother are arguing about it," I said.

"Another one?" Tumpkin said. "How many does that make?"

"Forty-eight," I said gloomily. "And we don't have even a tiny hint of what it is this time."

"I could try and find out for you," Tumpkin offered diffidently.

"Don't bother," I said. "Caliph Arenschadd takes better care of his list of curses than he does of the crown jewels. If you got caught, he'd probably slap four or five curses on you at once."

"He can't," Tumpkin said smugly. "They only work one at a time. And besides—"

"It's all *right*, Tumpkin," I said hastily. "We'll

find out soon enough what number forty-eight is; you don't have to risk moving yourself up the list."

"Well, actually—" Tumpkin said, and stopped, looking very uncomfortable.

"Tumpkin!" I said, staring at him. "Do you mean to say the caliph has never put *any* of his curses on you?"

"I guess so," Tumpkin said. "I mean, no, he hasn't."

"You must be really good at keeping out of the way," I said with considerable admiration. "I've never heard of anyone who didn't make it through at least five curses during his first six weeks at court, and you've been around for nearly a year!"

"Longer than that, but I spend a lot of time out here." Tumpkin sounded more uncomfortable than ever, so I let the subject drop and went back to talking about my parents and curse number forty-eight. After a while Tumpkin relaxed, but he didn't make a second offer to sneak a look at Caliph Arenschadd's list of curses.

I stayed with Tumpkin for most of the afternoon, and there was still no sign of the curse when I started for home. That worried me. The longer Caliph Arenschadd's curses take to have an effect, the nastier they tend to be. I could tell that Mother and Father were worried, too; neither of them said much at dinner.

That evening I had the first dream. I was running

and running through the night, and the wind was in my hair, and a silver moon shone high in the sky. I woke up just as I realized that I was running on four feet, like a dog. The thin crescent of the waxing moon was framed in the window at the foot of my bed. I sat staring at it for a long time before I fell asleep again.

I had the same dream the following night. I didn't worry about it much at the time; I was far more concerned about the forty-eighth curse. There still didn't seem to be any signs of it taking hold, at least none that I could see, and I'd never known one of Caliph Arenschadd's curses to take this long to affect someone. I stayed inside most of the time, figuring that I'd rather not have to try to get home with my feet turned backward or my knees stuck together if the curse hit all of a sudden. I didn't even go to the palace to see Tumpkin.

Two nights later, the dream got stronger. I ran and ran, with the wind down my back and the ground flowing past my feet and the sweet smell of grass at night in my nostrils. And a silver moon hung round and perfect in the sky above me.

I dreamed again the following night, and every night after that. Always it was the same dream, of running strong and free and wild in the wind and the moonlight. And always I woke with the moon shining through the window at the foot of my bed. At first it was just a crescent-shaped sliver of silver light, but every day the sliver grew wider. My dream became more and more vivid as the moon waxed, until I could close my eyes even in the day and see moonlight shining on sharp blades of grass. I began looking forward to the night, because I knew that then I would dream of running in the wind.

I didn't tell anyone about the dream. Mother and Father were still puzzling over the curse, and I didn't want to distract them. Besides, the dream was a private, special thing. I didn't want to share it with anyone, not even Tumpkin.

Not that I'd been seeing much of Tumpkin. At first I didn't go to the palace because I didn't want the curse to catch up with me while I was away from home. By the time I decided I didn't care about the curse, I didn't want to go anywhere. I probably would have stayed home forever if Mother hadn't chased me out after a week so she could work on some delicate enchantments.

Tumpkin was glad to see me. In fact, he practically pounced on me the minute I came into the garden. "You're back!" he said. "Did your parents figure out how to break it already? What was it, anyway?"

"What was what?" I asked crossly.

"The forty-eighth curse," Tumpkin said. He frowned worriedly at me. "Don't you remember?"

"Of course I remember!" I snapped. "No, Mother and Father haven't broken it, because they still don't know what it is."

"They don't know?"

"That's what I said. Didn't you listen? I think they should give up. If nothing's happened yet, the curse probably didn't take and we don't have anything to worry about."

"Something's happened," Tumpkin muttered.

"What did you say?" I said. "Why are you staring at me like that?"

"I said, something has happened," Tumpkin replied quickly. "Your eyebrows are getting thicker."

I snorted. "Well, if that's all curse forty-eight amounts to, I think Mother and Father should quit wasting time trying to break it. Who cares what my eyebrows look like?"

He didn't have an answer for that, so he told me about the latest book he was reading instead. I was feeling restless and impatient, but I knew Mother would be annoyed if I came home too early, so I made myself listen politely. At least I didn't have to say anything myself as long as Tumpkin was talking.

Tumpkin kept giving me speculative looks whenever he thought I wasn't looking. Finally I couldn't stand it any longer, and I left. I dawdled all the way home, and then when I arrived Mother and Father were talking and hardly even noticed me.

". . . beyond the bounds of reason this time," Mother was saying as I came in. "Even you have to admit that."

"I'm sure the caliph has a reason," Father said in

the stiff tone he uses when he knows he's wrong but can't say so.

"For a curse like this? We aren't talking about a petty inconvenience, Selim. This is a danger to everyone in the city. And there's no cure for lycanthropy."

"Caliph Arenschadd wouldn't endanger his people," Father said, even more stiffly than before.

"Maybe not if he thought about it first," Mother retorted. "But I don't think he's thought about this at all. Lycanthropy—"

"Imani!" Father said, spotting me at last. He shot Mother a look that was half warning, half relief. "When did you come in?"

"Just now," I said. I looked up at him. His eyebrows were getting thicker; they nearly met in the middle. Mother's were thicker, too. "What's lycanthropy?"

Mother and Father looked at each other. "You might as well explain, Selim," Mother said. "If we don't tell her, she'll just look it up in the dictionary."

Father sighed. "*Lycanthropy* means the assumption by human beings of the form and nature of wolves," he said, and looked down. "That's what the forty-eighth curse is, Imani. We've become werewolves."

"Well, I don't see what's so terrible about that," I said. I thought of my dream of running in the moonlight. "I think I'm going to like being a wolf."

They stared at me as if they'd never seen me before. Then Mother got a grim look on her face. "You'll find out soon enough," she said.

Mother was right. Two nights later I woke up well after midnight, feeling strange and tingly all over. I slipped out of bed and went out onto the balcony that overlooks our private garden. It was deep in shadow, because the moon was still on the other side of the house, rising. I could see the edge of the shadow creeping nearer as the moon rose, and I shivered in anticipation. I sat on the edge of the balcony, watching the line of moonlight come nearer, and waited.

The moon came over the domed roof of the house. I leaned into the silvery light and felt myself change. It was strange and exciting and scary all at once, though it didn't hurt at all. A moment later I stood on four paws and shook myself all over. Then I sat back and howled at the moon.

I heard answering howls from the corner of the house, and then two adult wolves came padding into sight below my window. Mother had turned into a slender, coal black female; Father was dark gray and more solidly built. He had white hairs in his muzzle. I leaped down from the balcony to join them, and Mother cuffed me with her paw. I snarled, and she cuffed me again. Then Father made a sharp barking noise and we turned. Together we jumped over the garden wall and into the city streets.

The first thing I noticed was the smells. The whole

city reeked of garbage and people and cooking spices and cats and perfumes. It was awful. I cringed and whined very softly. Mother bared her teeth in sympathy, and even Father coughed once or twice. Then we faded into the shadows and headed for the edge of town.

If it hadn't been for the smells, sneaking through the city like that would have been a lot of fun. As it was, I was glad we lived outside the city wall. Nobody saw us but a couple of dogs, and they ran when Father snarled at them. And then we passed the last of the houses and came out into the fields.

It was even better than my dream, to begin with. We ran and ran, and I could feel the wind in my fur and smell the fresh grass and the flowers and the little animals that had hidden as we approached. Now and then we'd stop and howl for the sheer joy of it. And all the while, the moonlight poured down around us in silver sheets.

Then we ran over the rabbit. Literally ran over it; the stupid thing was too scared to move when it heard us coming, and Father tripped over it. *Then* it ran, or rather, tried to. Mother caught it before it got very far. She trotted back with it while Father was picking himself up, and we split it between us.

The moon was getting low in the sky, and we began to feel a need to return home. I tried to fight it; I didn't want to go anywhere near that awful-smelling place again. But all I could do was whine and shuffle and edge closer. Mother cuffed me a couple of times because I wasn't going fast enough to suit her, and finally she nipped my tail. I yelped and gave up, and we ran back toward town.

As we passed the first house, we heard a baby crying inside. Mother and Father stopped and exchanged glances, just the way they'd done when they were people. Father looked up at the sky. The moon was close to setting; we had to get home. He growled and leaped forward, and Mother and I followed. A few minutes later, we reached our house and jumped over the garden wall.

Jumping back up to my balcony was harder than jumping down; I had to try twice, and I almost didn't make it in time. The moon set just as I scrabbled over the balcony rail, and I sprawled on the floor as a girl instead of a wolf. I sat up, remembering the wild run I'd just had.

Then I was sick to my stomach. Raw rabbit may be great when you're a wolf, but it's pretty disgusting to think about when you're a person.

I didn't get much sleep the rest of that night. I had too much to think about. I felt as if I'd been suckered: all those dreams about running in the moonlight, and not one about raw rabbit. I wondered how many other nasty surprises were in store for me. I thought of the way Mother and Father had looked at each other when they heard the baby cry. A cold shiver ran down my back, and I decided I didn't want to find out any more about being a werewolf. Then I remembered Mother's voice saying, "There's no cure for lycanthropy," and I shivered again.

Mother and Father were late to breakfast the next morning, and when they came in they were arguing. "It's the only thing we can do," Mother insisted. "And after last night, we have to do *something*. If Imani hadn't slowed us down coming home, that baby might have been—"

"There has to be another alternative," Father interrupted. He sounded desperate.

"Suggest one," Mother said. "Bearing in mind that the moon still isn't completely full, so we'll have at least another three or four nights like the last one unless we solve this problem right away."

I looked up. "Mother! You've found a way to break the curse?"

"Not quite," Mother said. "But we've come up with something we hope will work just as well."

I looked from Mother to Father. "What are you going to do?"

Father sighed. "I'm going to apologize to Caliph Arenschadd," he said reluctantly.

Mother insisted that both of us go along with Father to apologize to the caliph. I'm not sure whether she was worried about Father's ability to be tactful or whether she thought Caliph Arenschadd would be more likely to relent if he were faced with all three of us at once, but she was very firm. So I had to spend all morning having my hair washed and perfumed and my hands painted, and putting on my best clothes. Then I had to wait while Mother and Father finished doing the same things. I had to sit practically without moving so I wouldn't muss my hair or tear my skirts or rub any of the paint off my hands. I hate court appearances.

When we got to court, we were ushered into the caliph's presence for a private audience. Father bowed and started in on the obligatory courtesies. I didn't bother listening; all that O-Radiant-Light-of-the-Universe stuff bores me. I looked around the audience chamber instead, and that was why I saw Tumpkin sneaking in at the back. I stiffened. *Nobody* is supposed to be at a private audience except the caliph, whoever he's seeing, and the deaf guards the caliph hires especially for private audiences. Tumpkin would be in real trouble if anyone else noticed him.

Father finished his apology. "Very nicely put," the caliph said, smiling. "Accepted. Was there anything else?"

"O Commander of Legions, the curse yet remains," Father said delicately. "That is, the forty-eighth curse of your renowned list of curses, which you in your great and no-doubt-justified anger cast over me and my wife and daughter."

"Of course it remains," the caliph said. He sounded a little testy. "When I curse someone, they stay cursed until they break it."

"O Fountain of Wisdom, you have said it better than your humble servant ever could," Father replied. "That is our difficulty precisely. For nowhere in all the scrolls and tomes and works of magic is written the cure for your forty-eighth curse, and so we have come to you to beg your mercy."

"You want me to lift the curse, is that it?" the caliph said, frowning. "I don't like the idea; it would set a bad precedent."

Father wiped his forehead with the end of his sleeve. "O Auspicious and Merciful Caliph, what is wrong with establishing that a man's punishment ends when he humbly acknowledges his error? Display your justice before the whole court, and remove this dreadful curse from me and mine."

"Well . . ."

"O Just and Sagacious Monarch, let me add my entreaties to my husband's," Mother said. She stepped forward and knelt gracefully in front of Caliph Arenschadd. "Have pity! Or if your heart is hardened against us, think of your subjects who huddle within their doors each night in fear while wolves prowl the streets. Think of them, and lift the curse."

"Get up, Mirza, get up," the caliph said. "You know that sort of thing makes me uncomfortable."

"O Caliph of Compassion, I cannot," Mother said, bowing her head so he couldn't see the annoyance on her face. "My limbs will not support both my body and the curse that weighs on me. Lift the curse, and I will stand."

"I can't," said the caliph.

"What?" said Mother and Father together.

"I didn't work out how to lift all the curses I made up," Caliph Arenschadd said self-consciously. "I didn't think I needed to."

"You mean you were too lazy to bother," Mother muttered. Father gave her a horrified look, but fortunately Caliph Arenschadd hadn't heard.

"O Powerful Sovereign, what then are we to do?" Father said.

"You'll just have to find a way to break it yourselves," Caliph Arenschadd said. He was trying to sound airy and unconcerned, but I could see that he was really embarrassed and worried. He wasn't much better than Father at pretending he was right when he knew he wasn't.

"But Commander of Legions, there *is* no cure for lycanthropy!" Father said.

"Not usually," Tumpkin said from behind the caliph. "But I think I know one that will work this time."

I shut my eyes, wondering what Caliph Arenschadd would do to Tumpkin for sneaking into a private audience and whether Tumpkin would be able to tell us how to break the curse before Caliph Arenschadd did it. Nothing happened, so after a moment I opened my eyes again. Mother, Father, and the caliph were all staring at Tumpkin, who looked pleased and proud and a little embarrassed by all the attention he was getting. Nobody seemed to be angry.

"My son, how can this be?" said Caliph Arenschadd. "You are still a beginner in wizardry. How can you do what my grand vizier"—he waved at Father—"his skilled and intelligent wife"—he gestured at Mother—"and myself cannot achieve?"

"It's not wizardry, Father," Tumpkin said. "It's just logic."

" '*Father*'?" I said indignantly. "You mean you're the *prince*? Why didn't you *tell* me?"

"Imani!" Mother said sharply. "Mind your manners! Pray forgive the impulsiveness of her youth, Your Highness."

"It's all right," Tumpkin said. "We've known each other for a long time."

"You seem to have many secrets I was not aware of, my son," said Caliph Arenschadd, but he couldn't keep from sounding proud instead of reproachful. "Therefore, tell us how you think to break this curse."

"It's just a theory," Tumpkin said. "But you told me once that your curses only work one at a time. If you cast another curse on the grand vizier, wouldn't that take the place of this one?"

Mother and Father and Caliph Arenschadd all stared at Tumpkin some more. I stared, too, thinking furiously. If Caliph Arenschadd put the next curse on Father, we'd be in the same situation we'd been in when Father got the forty-eighth curse, not knowing what the curse was or how to break it. Curse forty-nine could be just as bad as all this werewolf business. But if somebody *else* made the caliph mad . . .

"That's the stupidest thing I've ever heard," I said loudly.

Everyone turned to look at me. Mother and Father looked horrified; the caliph looked startled and unbelieving. Tumpkin grinned, and I knew he'd figured out what I was up to.

"Imani!" Mother said automatically.

"What was that you said, girl?" Caliph Arenschadd asked ominously.

I swallowed hard and said, "I said that that list of curses was a stupid idea. And it was even stupider not to figure out how to break them all. Stupid and lazy. And sticking in a werewolf curse was the stupidest thing of all. *Everybody* knows you can't break a werewolf curse, but I bet you didn't even think about it."

I paused for breath. The caliph was positively purple with rage; the minute I stopped talking, he pointed three fingers at me and said something that sounded like "Donny-skazle frampwit!"

I looked at Mother and Father. They were bright green.

I heaved a sigh of relief; I hadn't been quite sure that Caliph Arenschadd would start over with the first curse on the list for me. I studied Mother and Father again, more closely. Their eyebrows were back to normal.

"It worked!" I said. I grinned at Tumpkin, then looked at Caliph Arenschadd. "Sorry about that, Your Majesty; I was just trying to make you mad."

"Imani . . ." Mother sounded as if she didn't know whether to laugh or scold me.

I shrugged. "Well, *somebody* had to do it. And I wasn't sure it would work right if the caliph wasn't really mad at somebody. 'Scuse me, Your Majesty."

"I believe I understand," the caliph said slowly. He looked from me to Tumpkin and back. "Just don't do it again, young woman. Audience concluded."

I went straight outside and walked backward around the palace three times, and that took care of being green. Then Mother and Father took me home and fussed over me. Father said I was quick-witted enough to make a fine diplomat, if I'd just learn a little tact, and he'd start my training tomorrow. Mother said that Father was a fine one to talk about tact, and she wasn't going to let him waste my abilities in politics. She was going to start teaching me sorcery that evening.

I left them arguing and went to see Tumpkin. He was waiting in the garden, just as I expected.

"You took awhile getting here," he said.

"My parents wanted to argue," I explained. "Why didn't you tell me you were the prince?"

"I didn't think you'd believe me," Tumpkin said. "I don't look much like a prince, you know."

I snorted. "What's that got to do with anything?"

"It seems to matter a lot to some people," Tumpkin said, and neither of us said anything for a little.

"How did you figure out what to do about the curse?" I asked finally.

"I don't know," Tumpkin said. "I just thought about it a lot, after I found out it was a werewolf curse. I knew it was going to take something unusual to get rid of it, or your mother and father would have figured it out weeks ago."

"They'd never have thought of getting rid of one curse by replacing it with another," I said.

Tumpkin looked at me sidelong. "Was it very bad?" he asked.

"Some of it," I said shortly, thinking of the rabbit and the way the city streets smell to a wolf. Then I thought about running through the grass. "Some of it was wonderful."

Tumpkin didn't ask any more questions, and he never has. I think he understands, but he won't make me tell him about the details until I want to. That's why we're such good friends. I still call him Tumpkin, even though now I know he's really the prince.

A couple of weeks ago Caliph Arenschadd issued a new proclamation about punishing people who offend him. He's decided to turn them blue. The more times someone offends him, the bluer they get and the longer it lasts. Father talked him into it by pointing out that it's rather difficult to do most of the jobs in the palace with your eyelids stuck shut or three-foot fingernails, but no one will have to stop working just because he's blue. So no one else will ever work up to curse forty-eight, and we won't ever have to worry about werewolves in town.

Which is a good thing, I suppose. But sometimes I still dream about moonlight and the wind in my fur as I run, and run, and run forever through endless, sweet-smelling grass.

CARTHWITCH

THE CAVE WAS DARK, damp, and smelled faintly of sulfur. After nearly seven years, Mariel knew every small unevenness in the floor, and she walked surely despite the darkness. Empty-handed, as was fitting, she crossed to the inner cavern, where only she was allowed to go. She paused at the threshold, checked by the weight of power and magic within. Then, slowly, she entered.

The water of the vision pool hissed and bubbled, heated by the lava flows deep within the mountain. Mariel stopped just short of the edge and knelt on the warm stone. Closing her eyes, she stilled her thoughts and emptied her mind. When she was ready at last, she opened her eyes and bent forward, peering into the steamy darkness to see what the earth magic would choose to show her.

Noon sunlight and a clear sky. Armies clashed on once-fertile fields, grinding the sprouting grain into dust and watering it with blood. In the distance a village burned, and the wailing of women and children made a faint counterpoint to the desperate clash of arms.

Mariel took a slow, deep breath, holding fast to her stillness as the scene played itself out. For six months now, this was all the earth magic had shown her: war; destruction; slave caravans hauling men, women, and children away from the ruins of their homes; the king's armies in retreat, or struggling to hold back the tide of the invaders long enough for the civilians to escape. The previous Earthwitch had assured her that behind each vision the earth magic showed, there was a purpose, but sometimes Mariel thought that if she did not find out soon what she was expected to learn from the death and destruction, she would go mad.

The vision changed. She saw the interior of a tent and a lean, brown-haired man in a chain vest, seated on the edge of a cot with his head buried in his hands. The tent flap opened. "My lord?" said a voice from outside.

The man on the cot looked up. Mariel choked, and the vision wavered; barely in time, she suppressed her unruly emotions. When her sight cleared again, the brown-haired man and a tired-looking man in a torn red cloak were in midargument.

"My lord, it is madness!" the man in the red cloak said.

"Have you some other proposal, then?" the brown-haired man asked with implacable skepticism.

The red-cloaked man shook his head. "But the ambassadors we sent to Wirnor have not yet returned. Surely, when they do—"

"We cannot wait for them," the first man said. "Not if we hope to have a people or an army left by the time they get here. We're running out of places to retreat to. We need a solution *now*."

"With all due respect, my lord, asking the Earthwitch for help is no reasonable solution. She is—"

In the cavern, Mariel's hands clenched into fists. Breathe in, breathe out; watch and listen now, study the meaning later. When her attention returned to the vision, she found that she had missed some of the red-cloaked man's argument.

"Nonsense," the brown-haired man snapped. "She's an old woman, as human as you or I. But she wields great power. If she can't stop the Dhainin with it, no one can. And in case it hasn't occurred to you, let me point out that if the Earthwitch puts an end to this invasion, we won't be indebted to Wirnor, which will make it a good deal easier to strike a favorable trade bargain next year or the year after."

"The Earthwitch does not care about such things. What if she refuses to help?"

"She won't refuse me."

The red-cloaked man looked startled. "My lord! You're not thinking of going *yourself?* In person?"

"I'm not thinking of it, no. I'm planning on it. And I'm going alone."

"My lord, you can't—"

"I can. I'll deal better with her alone, and anyway, we can't spare the men for an escort."

There was a moment's silence. Then the man in the red cloak bowed. "As you wish, my lord," he said with disapproving reluctance. "When do you leave?"

"In the morning. I've left instructions with Remin. You're in charge until I get back. If I don't come back—" He shrugged. "You're still in charge."

"I? My lord—"

The image faded to blackness, and the steamy sulfur smell of the vision cave rose strongly around her. Mariel drew a ragged breath, then another, and forced her cramped fingers open. So this was where the visions had been leading her! But was it to be her test, or his?

As she calmed, she turned the vision over in her mind. He had looked older—well, it had been fourteen years, it was only to be expected—but he was still the Evan Rydingsword she remembered, right down to the arrogant certainty in his tone and bearing when he said, "She won't refuse me."

Anger swept Mariel at the memory. Let him come and beg for her help. She *would* refuse. She would send him away empty-handed, and it would be only what he deserved . . . The visions of war and cruelty and death rose in her mind, and she stopped, considering. If the earth magic had intended her to refuse her help, would she have been shown all those other scenes? To help or not was not her choice, in any case. She could invoke the earth magic; she was the channel through which it flowed, but she did not wield it or control it. The earth did as it would. It was the first and hardest lesson her mentor had taught her.

Feeling calmer, she rose and started slowly back through the darkness. At least she knew he was coming; he would not take her by surprise. Suddenly her eyes went wide. Could he have discovered, somehow, that she was the Earthwitch now? Was that the reason for his arrogant confidence? She caught her breath. Did he think to use her, or perhaps even to take her back with him? And what would she do, if that was his intention? Pulling free of him had been the hardest thing she had ever done, harder even than learning to submit to the power of the earth. If he asked her to return, could she look him in the eyes and refuse?

Her seven years of service here were almost over. Soon a new man or woman would arrive, hoping to serve the earth magic, or perhaps only hoping, as she had, to escape from the past. After six months of training, she would hand over her office and leave Firewell Mountain. Most of the former Earthwitches went on to other kinds of service to the land and the people, as healers or wisewomen. Mariel had thought to teach in the great school for healers in Forralan, but if she were to go back with Evan instead . . . ? *Could* she go back?

Shaken and confused, she brushed past the two apprentices waiting outside the deep caverns and made her way to her apartments. Evan would not arrive for a few days yet. She had time to think . . . but not much of it.

With the weary determination of one who has no choice but to continue, Evan Rydingsword climbed the narrow trail on the side of Firewell Mountain. The wind sang around him, pulling at his cloak and chilling him to the bone. For a moment, he wondered whether he should have taken Corbin's advice and brought an escort. Then he shook his head. Without companions, he did not have the double burden of being exhausted and having to hide it. How long had it been since he had slept more than a few hours at a stretch? He could not recall.

As he pulled himself around a sharp bend in the trail, a figure moved out of the shadows. Automatically, his hand went to his sword hilt. Then he saw that it was a girl, hardly more than fourteen, dressed in a flowing brown robe.

"You have come to see the Earthwitch," she said with a calm certainty that seemed unnatural in one so young.

Evan blinked. "You are not the Earthwitch," he stated after a moment.

"I am her student. When I finish my training next year, I will be teacher and healer for my village. Now, I am to take you to the Earthwitch. Come." Without waiting to see whether he would follow, the girl turned and went lightly up the pathway.

Taking a deep breath, Evan followed. A few moments later, the trail ended, three-quarters of the way up the mountain. On the right, the rocks dropped to a dangerously sheer cliff. On the left, a dark opening gaped in the mountainside. The swordsman eyed it uncertainly, but the girl motioned to him to enter. Taking a deep breath, he did as she bade him.

Three paces inside, he stopped to allow his eyes to adjust. The cave was cool, and he could feel a dampness in the air that must mean water somewhere farther in. The girl plucked a small lamp from a niche beside the door and continued on with barely a pause; he had to hurry to catch up with her. The lamplight flickered and bobbed with her movements, making it hard to see, and he stumbled frequently on the uneven stone. The girl did not seem to notice or care, and Evan began to grow angry. Sternly, he reminded himself that he was here to ask for help, and forced his irritation down.

Finally, the girl paused before an iron door. "The Earthwitch awaits you," she said. "Enter, and do what you have come for."

Evan nodded, in thanks or farewell, he was not sure which, and opened the door. The cavern on the other side was better lit than the passageways, and he could make out more of his surroundings. In the center of the cavern, four columns like frozen rivers of stone framed a raised dais. On either side of the dais stood a brazier of black iron, filled with glowing coals. Behind them, half in shadow, sat a slender figure in a hooded robe who could only be the ancient Earthwitch.

Stepping into the glow of light from the braziers, Evan made a formal bow. "Lady, I thank you for your kindness in seeing me."

The hooded figure rose, surprising Evan with the grace of the movement. "You may thank me at the end of your visit, if you still feel you have reason," said a low, musical voice.

Evan went cold. That was not the voice of a crone, it was— He stood frozen in place as the woman stepped forward and put a small hand up to her hood.

"Welcome to Firewell Mountain, Evan Ryding-sword," said the Earthwitch, and put back the hood of her robe.

Her hair was still the color of sunlit grain; her eyes

the same clear, cold gray. Her face was more mature, but no less beautiful. He stared, unbelieving, and reached out blindly in her direction. "Mariel!" he whispered. "Oh, Mariel," and the room spun about him and went dark.

Mariel stared down at the unconscious man in dismay. Whatever she had expected from this confrontation, it was not this. She shook herself and clapped her hands for her students. "He has exhausted himself," she said when they appeared and exclaimed in astonishment. "We will take him to the visitor's chamber. Then, Veryl, you must make a broth, while Niza prepares the resting herbs."

The students nodded jerkily, eyes wide. Working together, they got Evan onto the bed; then the two girls vanished to follow Mariel's instructions, leaving her to watch over him.

In the clear, bright lamplight, Mariel could see that her words were truer than she had realized. Evan's face had a grayish cast beneath its tan, and the skin below his eyes was dark and bruised looking. Close up, she could see that his mail hung more loosely than it should have, and in several places the rings were broken or missing. He had not come to such a state in a five-day journey to Firewell Mountain. How had she missed seeing it before?

Almost without her willing it, her hand reached out to stroke his hair. She pulled it back before she touched him and shook her head. "Still you are a danger to me, Evan," she whispered, folding her hands tightly in her lap.

It seemed a very long time before Veryl and Niza returned.

Evan Rydingsword awoke lying on a hard, narrow bed. He tried to sit up, and a firm hand pushed him back. "Drink," a young female voice said, and he swallowed something warm. He shook his head and blinked at the figure above him. "Mariel?" he said doubtfully.

"I am here," said a voice from the shadows. She moved forward and nodded at the girl standing by Evan's bedside. "That is enough, Veryl; you may go."

The girl nodded and left. Evan barely noticed; he was staring at Mariel. She returned his gaze steadily.

"Where did you go?" he said at last. "Why did you leave?"

"Because I could not stay, and live."

His hand groped for his sword hilt. "Who threatened you? By the gods, if he still lives—"

For a moment, Mariel stared at him. Then she gave a brittle laugh. "No one threatened me, Evan. No one except you."

"I never threatened you!"

She shook her head. "You were swallowing me whole, you and your desire to be king. I tried to explain then, but you would not listen. Then you became king, and it was worse."

"I don't understand."

"I don't expect you to."

"I looked for you," he said bitterly. "I searched for months." He reached for her hands. "Mariel—"

She drew away, her face remote. "I am the Earthwitch now."

"And I am a king without a throne," Evan said. "Can we never be simply Evan and Mariel?"

"What brings you here?" Mariel asked, avoiding his eyes.

Evan closed his own for a moment, then looked up at her again. "The Dhainin."

She folded her hands in her lap. "Tell me."

"They came two years ago, from the southwest, raiding and burning. We drove them off, but they only returned in greater numbers. They have taken Saraset and burned Kerr Hollaran to the ground. I have fought them and lost, and fought again and lost again, until I have nothing left to fight with, and still they come. You are the only hope I have left."

"The Dhainin—"

"If we fight them, they seem to multiply until they overwhelm us with sheer numbers," Evan said wearily. "If we do not fight, they burn and slaughter anyway."

Mariel sucked in her breath. When he looked up she was staring into the air above the bed, as if she saw the same scenes of death and blood and burning that haunted his own dreams. "Perhaps," she said at last, reluctantly. "Perhaps something can be done. But there will be a price. There is always a price, even for you." She looked at him, and her eyes were shadowed. "Especially for you."

"Once I could have given you any treasure in the kingdom as your price." He looked at her. "Once, I would have."

"Gold is no price for the earth," she replied. "Birth and death, blood and healing, the slow changing of seasons—these are the coin for the earth magic. Whose life will you spend to buy your desire this time, king without a throne? A daughter? A son? Who will pay the price of the earth magic for you, so that you may have the victory and the kingdom when your war is over?"

Evan stiffened, stung by the bitterness of the accusation. "I have no sons. Nor daughters. Nor wife. All I can offer for the price of your magic is myself. And I am offering." As the words left his mouth, he found, to his surprise, that he meant them.

She stared at him in silence for a long time. Finally, she asked, "Why?"

"Because I am the king, throne or no," he said. "The people look to me to save them from the Dhainin, and while they wait, they die." His hands fists clenched in sudden anger. "They will die until the Dhainin leave, and I cannot make the Dhainin go."

"And that is all?"

"Isn't it enough? I have seen too much death. I want an end to this, Mariel."

She studied his face warily, as if she were not certain she believed him. Anger washed over him again, followed by a great weariness. "Do not toy with me," he said. "Will you help or no? Whatever I must do for it, I will."

"I, too, do what I must," she said, and he thought she sounded shaken. "I can promise you nothing. Tomorrow I will consult the fire and water; then you shall have your answer." Her raised hand cut off his protest. "Sleep now. You cannot hurry the times of the earth, and whether you have my help or no, you are in need of rest and food." She rose and vanished into the gloom of the cave.

Evan pushed himself up on one elbow and peered after her. If she had been only Mariel, his Mariel, he would have risen and followed her, but she was the Earthwitch now, and he did not quite dare. He dropped back to the bed and grimaced. Not dare? He had barely strength to hold himself up. To try to chase an unwilling woman through a dark maze of caves . . . he would not get three paces before he collapsed. He had kept moving out of necessity and will for so long that he had not realized how tired he had become. Mariel was right; he should sleep.

But he could not sleep. If Mariel—if the Earthwitch—agreed to help him, then he would pay for that help with his life. He had said it, and meant it, and he could not fool himself into thinking that the offer alone would be enough. Well, Corbin would be upset, but he would make a good king, and he had sons to follow him. A clear succession was important, or the substance of the kingdom was wasted on the sort of civil wars that had raged before he had taken the throne for himself.

Evan frowned. He had done what he could to assure that Corbin would have the throne if he did not return, but a king who vanished left doubts behind, no matter how good the preparations. Perhaps Mariel would let him send a message before he died. Mariel . . . His eyes closed at last, and he slept.

He was the same, and he was not. The arrogance was still there, but tempered in some way she did not understand. The old Evan would have demanded help and thought to haggle over the price; the old Evan would scarcely have noticed the pain of the people who died in his war.

He had changed, but not enough. If she went back to him, back to her old life, he would swallow her alive without even intending to. She could see it, feel it, in every look he gave her. She would fade to a shadow of his shadow, mouthing whatever words pleased him, and he would not even notice. Or perhaps this new Evan would notice, and be saddened, but he would never see how or why it had happened.

She could not go back. She did not dare. Oh, she wanted it—wanted him—more than she would have believed, even after all this time. But returning would mean losing all she had gained in the long, painful years—not her power as Earthwitch, for that was soon to end in any case, but her love of books and her knowledge of herbs; her fondness for sunrise and bird-song; her occasional pleasure in being alone; all the things, large and small, that made her herself and not a reflection of Evan Rydingsword and his ambition. She would lose them, because she knew she did not possess the strength to leave him twice.

"I am the Earthwitch," she said aloud, and the words echoed in the darkened cave, bringing her back to the present and the knowledge of her duties. She took a deep breath and set her fears and longings aside, as she had learned to set aside all her emotions when she invoked the earth magic. It was foolish to be concerned with such choices now. Evan had asked the earth for help; if that help were to be given, some price must be paid. Afterward, there would be time for other considerations, if the earth's demands had not made them impossible.

She set that thought aside, too, and rose from her chair. It was time to begin. Her tools were laid ready on the table before her: a small brazier of unlit charcoal, a cup of water from the pool of visions, flint and tinder, a clean cloth. Making a request of the earth magic was a more complex undertaking than accepting the visions it chose to show.

Clearing her mind of everything save Evan and the Dhainin, Mariel raised her arms and began the invocation. Her hands moved almost without conscious thought, lighting the fire, sprinkling the water, catching the flying ashes in the cloth. She sprinkled the fire again, sending more flecks of ash whirling upward with the steam, and breathed in the smoky scent. And knew before she opened the cloth what answer she would find there.

When Evan woke, Mariel was sitting beside his bed. Half dreaming still, he put out a hand, and she drew away. His hand dropped; she looked at him gravely.

"Are you determined?" she asked.

"What other choice do I have?"

"Then the earth magic will aid you," she said in a cool voice.

Evan sat up. "Thank you, Mariel."

"It is no doing of mine," she said sharply. "And the price is yet to be paid. You may still fail if you have lied about your motives." Evan did not reply, and after a moment she shook her head. "Come, then, if you are sure."

She led him through a dark and twisting passage, back to the pool where he had first seen her. At the iron brazier, she stopped and pointed. "Stand beside the pool," she said, "and do not move or look behind you until I tell you. Watch the water, and think of your purpose."

Evan stepped to the place she had indicated. A flicker of orange light glittered suddenly on the surface of the water and Mariel's voice began a harsh-sounding chant, but he did not turn. He sensed power slowly growing around him, until it surged in invisible waves, and he felt the very rocks were watching him. He stared at the water and thought of his dying men, his burning villages and war-torn land, and his own powerlessness.

The water became darker, reflecting nothing. Slowly it drew away from the center of the pool, and Evan saw something lying there, or growing, a shape blacker than darkness, darker than night: a sword. He did not move. He hardly dared to breathe.

Mariel's voice, the voice of the Earthwitch, rose behind him in a rasping command, then stopped. The water of the pool surged forward, then back, then forward again, and dull orange light from the brazier glittered on its surface once more. Outlined against the reflected light, the sword stood upright in the water, visible only as an interruption in the sparkling ripples. Hands reached past Evan, holding a cloth. A moment later, the sword had been pulled from the water, and a voice said, "You may turn."

Feeling as stiff and tired as if he had just fought a long battle, Evan looked away from the pool. His eyes met Mariel's blankly; then he saw the sword she held. It was made of black stone, dead black, the black of the center of the world where no light had ever fallen. He reached for it, and Mariel drew back.

"Not yet."

"That sword—"

"—is the means the earth has given you. The time for its use has not yet come. Veryl and Niza will see to you now. I have more preparations to make."

"Will I see you again before . . . whatever is to happen next?"

She hesitated, half turning. "Perhaps. Go now." With that, she vanished into the depths of the cave, carrying the stone sword carefully so that her cloth-wrapped hands would not touch its surface.

Two girls appeared in the doorway and escorted him back to the chamber where he had awakened. They brought him water and food, and he ate, trying to contain his impatience. He asked for, and received, writing materials and passed some time composing his letter to Corbin. He had nearly finished when Mariel returned.

"What is that?" she asked when she saw what he was doing.

"A letter to my chief commander." He signed it and stamped the bottom with his seal ring, then rolled the letter up and slipped the ring over the top. Finally, he tied them securely to the hilt of his sword and looked up. "Will you see that he gets this after . . . afterward?"

"I will arrange it."

"Thank you."

They sat for a few moments in silence. Then Evan said, "I thought I had a great deal still to say to you, but I find that two words cover most of it: I'm sorry."

"I, too."

"How much longer? Have you more preparations to make?"

"We can begin as soon as you are ready."

Evan swallowed hard and stood up. "I'm as ready as I can be, I think. But can you at least tell me what to expect?"

"No. I mean, I do not know myself. The earth does what it does, never twice the same, any more than two roses are identical, leaf for leaf. Whatever happens will rid your land of the Dhainin, but how, I do not know."

"Then let us go."

Mariel nodded and put up the hood of her robe. Silently, she gestured for him to follow and led him out into the maze of passageways. How long and how far they walked, Evan could not guess. At last they came to a flight of stairs, carved in rock, and Mariel led him upward.

They emerged abruptly into the pale golden sunlight of late afternoon. Evan blinked and looked about him. He stood on a narrow strip of barren earth. On one side, the mountain rose to its peak, shining in the sun; on the other, a lake of molten rock boiled and smoked between him and the edge of a cliff. Directly in front of him was a gray boulder with a flat top and on it lay the black stone sword. Seeing it, Evan took a swift step forward, then stopped in sudden doubt and glanced toward Mariel.

The dark green hood inclined in Evan's direction. Mariel's voice echoed strangely as she spoke, as if her words came from a great distance or through a long tunnel. "Evan Rydingsword, you have asked the aid of the earth magic to rid your country of the Dhainin. For this you came to Firewell Mountain; for this you have offered whatever the magic demands as the price of power. State now without fear: is this true?"

All the cruel tales of the Earthwitch and her magic rose in Evan's mind, and he hesitated. Other memories crowded in to match the tales, pictures of battle and burning. "It is true," Evan said, firmly putting his last doubts aside.

"Then step forward and take the sword of the earth, and let what will be, be so."

Evan walked slowly forward and reached for the hilt of the black sword. As he touched it, he saw Mariel—no, the Earthwitch—throw something toward the orange lake of fire. A cloud of smoke grew swiftly beside him, and in a moment he was surrounded by swirling, featureless gray. He lifted the sword.

Cold struck through his arm, and his eyes began to burn. The gray smoke cleared or became transparent in front of him. Looking through it, he saw, not the mountains, but a field, black with the Dhainin army. He shouted and held the sword aloft. Power ran down his arm in a wave of cold fire that continued on through him until it melted into the ground beneath his feet. A ripple of motion went through the Dhainin army, and then, with a terrible slowness, they began to sink.

Evan could not move, could not shout, could not even blink. With a fantastic clarity, he saw their faces twist in terror as the ground softened and the grassy earth rose around them. They sank with the slow inevitability of a pebble in a jar of honey, and when the surface of the plain closed at last above their heads there was no sign that they had ever existed.

Evan drew a single, shuddering breath—*I wanted the Dhainin gone, but no warrior deserves such a death*—and the scene changed. This time he saw a smaller group of Dhainin, strolling through the streets of a small town—Lemark, that was the place. He had lost it to the Dhainin barely two weeks before. Again he felt power run through him; again the earth softened beneath the feet of the men he saw, and they sank screaming into the cobbled street.

The scene shifted again, and again, until Evan hardly knew or cared what it was he watched. He tried to tell himself that the visions were unreal symbols, not images of actual events happening elsewhere, but with the earth's power surging through him he could not make himself believe it. Once the earth sucked down a troop of Dhainin raiders in the midst of a battle, leaving their opponents staring in fear and horror, and he recognized some of his rear guard.

At last the visions ended, and Evan felt the power fade. Slowly, he lowered the sword, and the gray smoke swirled tiredly, thinned, and dissolved. His people were safe, but he felt no triumph. There was no honor or glory in killing helpless victims, and the destruction of an entire people in such a way left him sick at heart, as no battle had ever done. He turned and saw Mariel standing at the edge of the cliff, her hood pushed back and her hair blowing in wisps around her face.

And the sword moved in his hand.

Evan looked down, stunned, and saw the stone sword rise, pulling his hand upward and forward. Pulling him toward Mariel. He cried out and tried to drop the sword, but his fingers would not obey him. He looked up and saw Mariel with the same unnatural clarity as he had seen the Dhainin. She watched for a moment, her face calm and grave, while the sword pulled him inexorably closer. Then, smiling slightly, she stepped forward to meet him.

Horror swept him; whatever price he had expected to pay, this was not it. He fought the pull of the black stone sword, but it was too strong. Left-handed, he groped for his own sword, but it was still in the sleeping chamber with his letter. His dagger, then. He drew it with difficulty. "I will not kill her," he said between clenched teeth, and slashed at his right wrist.

The steel cut cleanly through in spite of the awkward angle of the blow. Too late, Mariel cried out in protest, echoing Evan's scream of pain. The black stone sword hung in the air for another instant; then it fell and shattered on the ground at his feet. As the stone broke, he felt the power that had filled him break apart, and the vision of Mariel shattered like a picture in a breaking mirror. The shards of power and vision stabbed at his eyes, and he fell forward, the stump of his right arm gushing redness across the broken bits of black stone.

He woke in darkness with a throbbing pain in his right arm. He was lying on a rough, uncomfortable surface, and he could hear movement beside him. "Mariel?" he said weakly.

"I am here. I have bound your arm, and you will not bleed to death, but you need more tending than I can give you here. Can you walk back to the caves? I am afraid you are too much for me to carry."

"If you light the lamp so I can find the stairs, I think I can manage," Evan said.

"Light the lamp? But—" Mariel stopped, and Evan felt suddenly cold.

"Mariel, how long was I— How long has it been?"

"Not long."

"Not long," Evan repeated, peering vainly into the darkness. "Then—" But he could not finish. He felt more than heard Mariel move beside him and knew she was nodding.

"Yes. I should have seen before. You are blind, Evan." Her voice shook.

"Ah." He closed his eyes. "Well, take my life, then. It is the price I agreed to, and it is no longer much hardship to pay."

"No, Evan. The earth magic does not want your death, but your life." Her voice sank almost to a whisper. "I tried to warn you that there would be a price."

"The price was you!" Evan shouted. "Why else do you think I did this?" He tried to raise the stump of his arm and nearly fainted again from the pain.

"You crippled yourself because you were already blind," she answered, and he could hear the ring of power in her voice and knew that she spoke as the Earthwitch and not only Mariel. "You would not see what the earth tried to show you, so now you do not see at all. The price of the magic is your life and service."

"Like this? Blind and crippled?" he spat. "How can I live like this?"

"You must learn." The voice was gently implacable. "I will help you, if I can. But live you must. You are the earth's, now."

"You cannot help me rule," Evan said. "Even if I could persuade the people to accept a cripple as king—"

"You still do not understand," Mariel said sharply. "You are a king no longer. Your life belongs to the earth; when you are recovered and have sufficient training, you will become the next Earthwitch."

"You would have me be a blind mage." He snorted. "No."

"What the earth has taken, the earth can restore, if you accept what it shows you," Mariel said. "In any case you have no choice in this."

She hesitated, and the echo of the Earth magic faded from her voice. When she continued, he heard only Mariel. "It is not forever. You will serve seven years, as I have. When you have trained your successor, you will be free. And then—"

"And then?" He felt a wisp of hope.

"And then perhaps we will both be strong enough to be simply Evan and Mariel," she said slowly, as if the thought was so new to her that she must test each word as she spoke it.

Evan felt a hand on his good arm. Reluctantly, he let Mariel help him up and lead him carefully to the stairs.

THE SWORD-SELLER

THE TINY SWORD-SELLER'S BOOTH was almost hidden behind a row of tinker's stalls and jewelry stands; Auridan very nearly passed by without seeing it at all. When he did notice it, he paused. Then he shouldered his way toward it with a smile. He needed a sword, and half the fun of a fair was hunting bargains in the smaller booths.

The booth's proprietor, an old man in a dark blue robe, looked up as Auridan ducked under the awning. Auridan braced himself for the usual exhortations, but the man regarded him with a silent, unblinking stare. Auridan gave a mental shrug and bent over the counter. He was surprised at the disorder he found; knives, daggers, and swords of all lengths were jumbled as randomly as a child's game of catch-straws. Some had sheaths, some did not; some were polished and sharpened, others were black with age. A cursory glance was enough to tell Auridan that nothing here was likely to be worth haggling over. He shrugged again and turned to go. As he did, a glint of color caught his eye.

Auridan stopped. A blue stone winked at him through a gap in the crisscrossed pile of weapons. Auridan moved two swords and four daggers and uncovered an ancient short-sword without a sheath. The blue stone was one of a pair set in the hilt, amid carving so clogged with grime that it was impossible to determine what the decoration represented. The blade of the sword was black with age, and thicker and wider than those Auridan was used to. Almost in spite of himself, Auridan lifted the sword, testing the heft. The hilt fit his hand as if it had been made to measure, and the balance of the blade was perfect.

"That sword is not for sale," a harsh voice rasped.

Auridan started and looked across the counter into the unfathomable eyes of the sword-seller. "If it is already spoken for, you should not display it with the rest of your wares," Auridan said in mild annoyance. He twisted the blade from side to side, studying it with regret. It would be a deal of work to clean and sharpen, but something about the weapon called to him . . . He shook himself and held the sword out to the sword-seller.

The old man made no move to take it from him. "I did not say the sword was spoken for," he said.

"No, I suppose you didn't," Auridan replied with a smile. "But what else am I to think when you refuse to sell it?"

"Think as you will," the man said, "so long as you do not think to buy that sword."

"As you will," Auridan said. Again he held out the sword. The old man sat watching him with the same unblinking stare.

"Very well, then." Auridan set the sword down gently atop the welter of other weapons in front of the old man. His fingers uncurled reluctantly from the hilt, and as he stepped away from the counter he was surprised to find that his breathing had quickened. "Good day, and fortune follow you," he said, and turned away.

"Wait."

Auridan looked back, but kept one hand poised to lift the fringe of the awning. "What is it?"

"The sword is not for sale. It is given. Today, it is given to you. Take it."

Auridan stared. Was the old man mad? Even an old and battered sword was worth a good deal, and this weapon was well made. The sword-seller looked as though he could make good use of whatever coin it would bring. "Why would you give me the sword?"

"That is my affair," the old man said. "The sword is yours. Take it."

Auridan heard finality in the sword-seller's voice, and the man's eyes were bright and knowing. They did not look like the eyes of a madman. Auridan reached for the hilt of the sword, then hesitated. Whatever the reason for this strange offer, he could not take such advantage of an old man. His hand went to the pouch at his belt and removed half of the scanty coins remaining. He held them out to the sword-seller. "Here. It's not the worth of such a weapon, by any means, but—"

"The sword is a gift!" the old man snapped. "Did I not say it?"

"I'll take it as a purchase, or not at all," Auridan said. Briefly, he wondered if he had not run as mad as the old sword-seller. Forcing a merchant to take coin at a fair! Whoever heard of such backward bargaining?

The old man snorted. "Take the sword and go."

Auridan shrugged. He tossed the coins onto the counter, where they made tiny noises as they clinked against the jumbled weapons and fell into the spaces between them. Only then did he put his hand to the hilt of the ancient sword.

"For your courtesy, I give thanks," Auridan said, and picked up the weapon.

He thought he saw a flash of worry in the

sword-seller's eyes. Then the man said, "You are a blank shield. I am sometimes asked to recommend such men to those who seek to hire them. If someone asks, where shall I send him?"

Auridan blinked in surprise, but said courteously that he could probably be found in the serving tent after sunset. He thanked the man and left, wondering why he had bothered. He doubted that anyone would seek to hire a mercenary by such roundabout methods. Still, he thought the suggestion had been well meant. He put the matter out of his mind and began looking for a leather-maker's booth where he could buy a sheath for the sword.

For the next several hours, Auridan strolled among the booths and tents, enjoying the warm sunshine and watching the eager, noisy crowds. The annual Fyndale fair had been resumed shortly after the end of the long war with the Hounds of Alizon, and it had grown every year since. Ten merchants' flags had flown above the booths at that first fair; now, four years later, there were thirty or more, and the tents and carts and tables of the lesser tradesmen sprawled in a disorderly semi-circle around the gray stone pillar where men swore to keep the peace of the fair.

Auridan remembered that first fair well. Unlike so many of his erstwhile comrades in the war against Alizon, he'd been restless and disinclined to settle down. By a lucky chance, he'd met one of the lords from the south who'd been dispossessed during the war. Auridan had taken service with him, and they had spent several years fighting in the southern part of High Hallack. Eventually, the lord and his men had prevailed, but the substance of his keep had been wasted in the struggle, and Auridan was not of a mind to squat there waiting for the man to rebuild his fortune. He had taken the lord's blessing, and the few coins that could be spared, and come back to Fyndale in search of another patron.

He studied the crowd as he walked along, and for the first time began to doubt the wisdom of the decision he had made with such blithe confidence. Most of the fairgoers looked prosperous and contented— good signs for the merchants, perhaps, but not so promising for a blank shield mercenary looking for someone in need of a guard or a soldier.

Well, if nothing else, he could hire on with a merchant returning home from the fair, Auridan thought philosophically. Merchants were notoriously nervous about bandits, particularly when there were profits to protect, and from the look of things, this fair would be profitable for nearly all of them. Feeling somewhat more cheerful, Auridan headed toward the serving tent, to purchase a cup of wine and consider what to do next.

Two drinks later, he had still not thought of anything. He was just beginning his third when a light, musical voice said, "Fair fortune to you, traveler. Are you the blank shield the sword-seller told me of?"

Auridan looked up, and his reply died on his lips. The woman who stood beside him had the kind of beauty songsmiths broke their strings over. Her thick, butter-colored braids coiled into a high knot above a classic oval face. Her skin was fair and flawless, her eyes a serene hazel. She was tall and slender, and her cloak and robe were of fine wool, heavily embroidered. She could be no more than twenty, but her bearing proclaimed a confidence beyond her years.

She must be daughter to one of the Dales lords, Auridan thought dazedly; then his bemused wits began working again and he rose to his feet and raised his hand palm-out in greeting. "Fair fortune to you, lady. I am Auridan; how may I serve you?"

The woman's lips compressed very slightly; then she sighed and motioned for Auridan to seat himself once more. She took the place beside him and said, "I wish to hire a man to guide and guard me on a journey. I have been told that you are a man of honor and would suit my purposes."

"I have done such work before," Auridan admitted. "What direction do you travel and with how large a party?"

The woman bit her lip and looked down; suddenly she seemed much younger, barely out of girlhood. Then she raised her chin and said defiantly, "I wish to go north, to Abbey Norstead. And the party will consist of we two only; I will take no others with me." She added solemnly, "It is why I particularly wish to hire an honorable man."

Auridan swallowed a chuckle, but shook his head. "I fear you have not considered, lady," he said gently, even as he wondered why such a girl as this would wish to enter the abbey. "The effects of the war linger; travel is still not safe. I cannot believe your kinsmen would allow—"

"The last of my kin by blood is at Abbey Norstead," the girl broke in pointedly.

"Then you'd do far better to stay in Fyndale for a week or so, until the fair ends, and hire passage in a merchant's train. I'm sure that at least one or two will head toward Norsdale."

"I've no mind to wait so long," she retorted. "Nor do I wish to move at a snail's pace, stopping at every village and hamlet in hopes of another sale."

"I see you've journeyed with merchants before," Auridan said, amused.

"Two travelers alone may well be safer than a larger group," she persisted. "For two can hide, or slip away silently in darkness, where more cannot."

"A single guard may also be easily taken by two or three outlaws, who would never think to attack a stronger party," Auridan pointed out. "And with such a one as you to tempt—"

"I am not helpless!" she interrupted angrily. "I know the use of a sword, though I am better with a bow."

Without thinking, Auridan raised a skeptical eyebrow. The girl saw, and her eyes flashed. "You think that because I am beautiful I have no thoughts in my head save silks and jewelry, and no skill in my hands but embroidery!" she said scornfully. "Faugh! I'm sick to death of men who see nothing but my face!"

Before Auridan could answer, a man's voice cut across the hum of talk surrounding them. "Cyndal! There you are at last!" The girl stiffened, and Auridan looked around for the source of the cry.

He found the speaker quickly—a tall, brown-haired man of perhaps thirty years, dressed in a tunic of fine crimson wool. He was making his way quickly through the crowd, his eyes fixed on the girl beside Auridan. "Hervan," the girl muttered, and she spoke as if the name were a curse. "He would!"

The brown-haired man reached the table. He ignored Auridan and said in a chiding tone, "My dear Cyndal! What do you here, and in such company? My lady has been frantic since she found you missing!"

"I don't believe you, Hervan," the girl replied, unmoved. "Chathalla knew I was going out, and I've barely been gone an hour. She wouldn't fuss over such a thing."

"Chathalla's nerves are particularly fragile just now," the brown-haired man said defensively.

"Your concern for your lady wife does you credit," Cyndal said in a dry tone.

"I could wish you had had as much consideration. What she will say when she knows where I found you . . ." He glanced disapprovingly around the serving tent, and his eyes came to rest on Auridan.

"Don't tell her," Cyndal suggested.

"Don't be ridiculous, Cyndal. You shouldn't be wandering around the fair alone; you know that. Come on, I'll take you back to the tent."

"I haven't finished my discussion with Auridan," Cyndal said.

"Cyndal, be reasonable!"

Hervan's tone was patronizing, and Auridan felt a wave of dislike for the young Dales lord. He decided to intervene. "But she is," Auridan put in pleasantly. "Being reasonable, I mean."

Hervan stared at him in blank astonishment, and Auridan gestured at the cup of wine he had been drinking. Fortunately, it was still three-quarters full, and he had set it down between Cyndal and himself, so that it was impossible to tell to which of them the cup belonged. "My lady has not yet finished her wine. Surely you do not think it would be reasonable for her to leave it behind?"

"Indeed." Hervan looked from Auridan to Cyndal, and the question in his expression was clear. Cyndal's lips tightened, but she presented Auridan as graciously as if they were at the court of one of the High Lords of the Dales instead of in a serving tent at a fair. She did not, Auridan noticed, mention what she had been discussing with him.

Hervan's expression cleared before Cyndal was half finished with her explanation. "A blank shield? How fortunate! I am in need of a Master of Arms; come to me tomorrow and we'll talk of it."

"Why, thank you, my lord," Auridan said, forcing his lips into a smile. "Tomorrow evening, perhaps? I would not wish to interfere with your fairing."

"I will look for you then," Hervan promised. "Now, Cyndal—"

"But Lady Cyndal still has not finished her wine," Auridan cut in smoothly. "Surely it won't matter if she stays here a little longer. I will be happy to escort her back if you wish to return and reassure your lady wife."

Hervan hesitated visibly, but he could not refuse without giving the impression that he did not trust Auridan. That would make Hervan look foolish, since he had just offered to take Auridan into his service. Hervan bowed graciously, showered Auridan with insincere thanks, and left at last.

Auridan turned to Cyndal. She was looking at him with an expression of mingled resignation and scorn, and he wondered whether she thought he had believed Hervan's playacting. "I think that now I understand exactly why you wish to go to Norstead," Auridan said before she could speak. "But I thought you said that you had no kin outside the abbey. Lord Hervan does not act like a stranger."

Cyndal's eyes widened; then, suddenly, she smiled. Auridan swallowed hard. Cyndal had been lovely before, but the glowing expression of relief and gratitude increased her beauty tenfold.

"Hervan was my uncle's stepson," Cyndal said, and Auridan gave himself a mental shake. He *had* asked, after all. "When my uncle saw that he was unlikely to have children of his own, he made Hervan his heir. Hervan has been lord in Syledale since my uncle died two years ago."

"And it took you two years to decide that you'd rather enter an abbey than live in his household?" Auridan said skeptically.

She laughed, but her expression sobered quickly. "No, it's only in the last few months that he's been acting that way, since he's known Chathalla will bear him an heir after Midwinter. I decided on the way to Fyndale that it would be easier on everyone if I went away for a while. My mother's sister at Abbey Norstead is the only blood relation I possess, so it's reasonable for me to go there."

Auridan stiffened as wild speculations chased each other through his mind. If the impending birth of an heir had triggered Hervan's subtle persecution of his cousin-by-marriage, Hervan's actions might well be rooted in something deeper than mere distaste for Cyndal's presence. And whatever the cause, it was certainly not a safe situation for a mercenary to become involved in. He opened his mouth to tell Cyndal as much, and found himself saying, "Have you told Lord Hervan of this plan of yours?"

"Not yet," Cyndal admitted. "I thought I would have a better chance of persuading him if Chathalla and I had all the arrangements made before I spoke to him of it."

"I see." Auridan was more confused than ever. "And she agreed to your traveling with a single man-at-arms?"

"I didn't mention that," Cyndal said. "She'd worry. I'll just tell her, and Hervan, that you've agreed to be my guide and head the men who'll accompany me. They won't think to ask how many men there will be."

"Why the need for all this subterfuge? Why don't you just take the five or six men you need with you?"

"Because Hervan wouldn't provide them, and I can't afford to hire that many!" Cyndal snapped. "And if you aren't going to help me, I don't see why I should answer any more of your questions."

"In that case, I shall escort you back to your cousin," Auridan said, rising. "I strongly recommend, however, that you explain matters to Lord Hervan before you approach me or anyone else on this subject again."

"That can be no concern of yours, since you do not wish to take me to Norstead," Cyndal said coldly as she rose to follow him.

Auridan scowled at her. "By the Nine Words of Min, lady, do you not realize how much trouble you would make for any man like me who accepted your offer unknowingly? Blood-kin or no, Lord Hervan stands as your protector! Were I to agree to take you to Norstead without his permission, I'd have to go on into the Waste and earn my bread by scavenging, for no lord would hire me afterward."

"Oh." Cyndal's voice was thoughtful, and she was silent for a long time. They had nearly reached the visitors' tents when she said, "I'm sorry; I hadn't thought of it that way. But if Hervan agrees, will you guide me?"

"Certainly," Auridan replied, then wondered whether the wine had not been stronger than he had thought. He gave a mental shrug. Time enough to worry once the girl got Lord Hervan's agreement to her plans; from what Auridan had seen, it did not look probable.

Cyndal did not appear to share Auridan's doubts. "Thank you," she said with a smile that took his breath away. "You are coming to speak with Hervan tomorrow, are you not? I'll talk to him before then."

Auridan nodded absently, and she directed him toward one of the tents on the outer perimeter of the camp. They finished their walk in silence, except for the obligatory courtesies exchanged when he returned her officially to her step-cousin's care. Then Auridan hurried away to his own campsite, feeling unreasonably relieved and irrationally anxious at the same time.

To give himself something to think about besides Cyndal, Auridan spent the evening worrying at the hilt of his new sword with polishing cream, strong soap, and a pile of old rags. He worked slowly to keep from accidentally dislodging the stones in the hilt. Even so, by the time he was ready to sleep he had removed most of the ancient grime from the carving that decorated the hilt. In the flickering firelight, all he could tell was that the two stones were the eyes of some wild-haired creature. Reluctantly, Auridan sheathed the sword, telling himself he could examine it more closely in the morning.

When he awoke, his first action was to reach for the short-sword. He was surprised to see how different the carving looked in daylight. The blue stones were indeed eyes, but what he had taken for hair was a crest of intricately carved feathers that stood out around the head of a serpentlike creature. The serpent's body twisted around the hilt of the sword, forming a series of ridges that made the sword less likely to slide in the hand. Auridan studied it, wondering from what tale the swordsmith had taken such a creature. A snake with feathers was strange enough to be a relic of the Old Ones . . .

Auridan shivered, then shook his head and smiled. The Dales were full of strange things left behind by the Old Ones, but one did not find them for sale at out-of-the-way booths in Fyndale. For while the leavings of the Old Ones might be dangerous indeed, there was always someone eager to take the risk in hopes of the power he might gain. Any merchant daring enough to traffic in such items would be charging enormous sums for them, not giving them away to mercenaries. Auridan pushed the remnants of his uneasiness to the back of his mind and went off to get himself some breakfast.

When he finished eating, Auridan took the sword to a busy tinker's stall and had the blade cleaned and sharpened. It cost more than he had expected, but it was worth it to have a good sword at his belt again. He spent the day wandering through the fair, but as soon as the sun disappeared behind the mountains he headed for Lord Hervan's campsite.

The guard who greeted Auridan did not seem surprised by his request to speak with Lord Hervan, and he was immediately ushered into one of the tents. He found Hervan, Cyndal, and a quiet, gentle-faced woman seated on small folding stools inside. Hervan rose, frowning, as Auridan entered.

"This is my wife, the Lady Chathalla," Hervan said, gesturing at the unfamiliar woman beside Cyndal. He paused, studying Auridan, then said abruptly, "My cousin claims she wishes to hire you to take her to Norstead."

"She mentioned the possibility," Auridan said

cautiously. He saw Cyndal shift, and Chathalla put a restraining hand on her arm, and he wondered what he had walked into this time.

"Indeed." Hervan's voice was barely a fraction friendlier. "And you approve of this proposal?"

Auridan raised an eyebrow. "Approve? My lord, I am a mercenary. I approve when I am paid."

Hervan gave a bark of laughter. "Very good. Sit down, then, and we'll talk."

As Auridan turned, looking for a fourth stool, he heard a short, hissing intake of breath. He straightened hurriedly. Hervan was staring at the carved hilt of Auridan's short-sword, and his expression was curiously blank. "My lord?" Auridan said cautiously.

Hervan ran his tongue over his lips. "The decoration of your sword hilt is . . . quite unusual."

"Really? I had thought it some whim of the smith who made it," Auridan said. "Have you seen similar work before, Lord Hervan?"

"Possibly." Hervan's tone was carefully casual, but his lips were stiff with tension. His eyes darted up to Auridan's face, then as quickly away. "Enough. What is your price for escorting my cousin to Norstead?"

Auridan blinked, somewhat bewildered by this abrupt change in attitude, then named a sum he knew to be reasonable. Hervan nodded, but he did not look as if he was devoting much of his attention to Auridan's words. Instead, Hervan was watching Cyndal, and after a moment he said almost pleadingly, "You're sure you want to take this trip, Cyndal? You won't change your mind?"

"Yes, I'm sure, and no, I won't change my mind," Cyndal said.

Hervan glanced at Auridan again and said heavily, "Very well. You wanted to leave tomorrow morning, didn't you? I'll see that everything is ready."

"You mean, you'll let me go without any more arguing?" Cyndal said, amazement and disbelief warring in her voice.

"I've no choice!" Hervan swung around to face her. He sounded desperate, and angry, and somehow frightened. "Cyndal . . ."

"What's wrong, Hervan?" Cyndal asked almost gently.

Hervan hesitated, and his wife leaned forward and said quietly, "Yes, please tell us."

Hervan jerked as if he had been stung, and his expression hardened. "Nothing. Nothing whatever." He looked at Auridan and said, "I'll have your payment ready in the morning."

Auridan nodded, and the bargain was swiftly concluded. He bowed his thanks and left, puzzling over the implications of the little scene. Hervan had all the earmarks of a badly frightened man, but why would the design of Auridan's sword hilt have frightened him? Auridan kicked at a rock in frustration. Hervan was lord of a Dale, however small; there was nothing Auridan could do to make him explain.

Briefly, Auridan considered leaving the sword behind, but he needed a weapon and he could not afford to buy another. Nor could he refuse to escort Cyndal, however uneasy her step-cousin's attitude made him. Even if he had not given his word to both Hervan and Cyndal, Auridan could not afford to pass up such a commission. His purse was nearly flat, and it would be at least a week before he could expect any income from an alternate position, supposing he could find one quickly. Auridan grinned suddenly. It was pleasant to have honor and necessity in agreement, for once, about his future course of action.

They left early the following morning, before the fairgoers emerged from their tents to crowd the space around the booths. Lord Hervan had provided a pretty chestnut mare for Cyndal that Auridan thought would be more than a match for his own gray. Hervan had also arranged saddlebags full of supplies for both Cyndal and Auridan, and he had a purse with Auridan's fee ready and waiting. He even suggested a route—the old track near the top of the ridges. Auridan thanked him without mentioning that he had been intending to take the high trail anyway. At this time of year, any outlaws would be watching the main road for unwary merchants; the high trail would be far safer for so small a party. Hervan's farewells to his step-cousin were perhaps a little stiff, but Auridan had to admit that in everything else the man had done as much or more than he had promised.

Cyndal was in a sober mood after taking leave of her cousin, and for the early part of the morning she rode in silence. But the warmth of the day and the cheerful calling of the birds proved too much for her to resist, and by the time they stopped for a midday meal she was laughing and talking with Auridan as though he had stood guard over her cradle.

Auridan was surprised at how comfortable he was with her. His previous experience with noblewomen had not led him to expect anything remotely resembling this casual camaraderie. Before he thought, he said as much, and Cyndal grinned.

"You've probably only seen proper noblewomen, like Lady Chathalla," she said without rancor. "Penniless females like me aren't usually allowed out in public."

"*Do* the Dales hold any other women 'like you'?" Auridan asked, studying her with exaggerated admiration.

"Hundreds," Cyndal said, and her smile faded. "I'm one of the lucky ones. If Chathalla weren't so nice, I'd have been stuck in the kitchens or the back gardens with fewer prospects than a serving wench. I've seen it happen; Uppsdale isn't very far away, and I remember how Lady Annet treated Ysmay. And Ysmay had dowry enough to marry, in the end; I don't even have that."

"Surely your uncle—" Auridan stopped short as he realized that, camaraderie or not, this was not the sort of question a blank shield ought to ask of a noblewoman.

"My uncle didn't think of settling anything on me for a dowry," Cyndal said. "He was more concerned with making sure no one would be able to object to Hervan as heir. And it was lucky he did; things were rather difficult for a while after he died. If he hadn't made such a point of Hervan's being his heir, blood-kin or not, I'm not sure what would have happened to any of us."

Auridan nodded sympathetically and changed the subject. He had seen enough in recent years to be able to guess more than he wanted to know about what Cyndal was not saying. The thought of this beautiful girl helplessly caught up in one of the sometimes bloody struggles over a Dales rulership made him wince. Then he smiled at himself. Beautiful Cyndal might be, but helpless? Little as he knew her, he knew she was not that.

Despite his enjoyment of Cyndal's company, Auridan grew increasingly uneasy as the day wore on. In the late afternoon, clouds began sweeping in from the west, turning the day gray and adding to his irritability. Finally Cyndal noticed his nervousness and demanded to be told what was wrong.

"I won't be treated like a porcelain ornament," she said. "And I can be dreadfully stubborn. So you might as well explain what's bothering you, and save us both the trouble."

"If I knew what it was, I'd tell you," Auridan replied. "It's just a feeling, that's all."

They rode until just before dark. A cold drizzle began to fall as they struggled to set up camp in the gloom, and they heard the rumbling of thunder among the nearby mountains. Auridan rigged an inadequate shelter for Cyndal from seven leafy branches and a blanket, then was exasperated when she insisted on joining him in hunting firewood.

The storm hit with a crash while they were heading back toward their camp with the second load. Rain slashed through the branches of the trees above them, soaking their cloaks in minutes and half blinding them. Auridan shouted to Cyndal to keep close; in the dark and the rain it would be all too easy to become separated and lose the way. He thought he heard Cyndal shout agreement, but a few moments later, a brilliant flash of lightning showed her forging through the trees ahead and to his right.

The thunderclap that followed drowned out Auridan's call. Cursing, he blundered toward where he thought she was. He ran into a tree and lost several of the branches he was carrying. As he struggled to get a better grip on those that remained, he heard Cyndal scream.

Auridan dropped the firewood and leaped forward. The scream had come from just ahead of him; he ought to be able to find her easily enough. He heard Cyndal scream again, and another flash of lightning lit the woods.

By its light, Auridan saw Cyndal plunging wildly into the trees. Just behind her, its head a man-height above the ground, was a creature with a long, sinuous body like a giant snake covered with feathers. Auridan grabbed for his sword as the light faded, and forced his feet to move faster. The image of the enormous snake hung before his eyes, as though the lightning had etched the scene into their surface. Then he realized that the snake was glowing. It moved forward without hurry, following Cyndal.

Auridan stumbled after it, determined to reach the snake before it could harm Cyndal. The chase seemed to last for hours, the darkness punctuated by occasional flashes of lightning. Auridan was grateful for the storm; the brief flares of light were the only way he had of being sure the snake had not yet reached its prey.

Suddenly the snake disappeared, like a puff of smoke scattered by the wind. Almost at the same moment, Auridan heard Cyndal give another scream. Desperately he threw himself forward. He had an instant's confused impression of plunging through something like a thin curtain into dryness and warmth and flickering torchlight, and then he collided with Cyndal.

They teetered together in a tangle of dripping hair

and soggy cloaks. Auridan recovered first and instinctively raised his sword. Then what he was seeing finally penetrated, and he stared in astonishment.

He was standing just inside a curtain of blackness that blocked the mouth of a huge cave. Torches burned in iron sconces hanging from the walls of the cave. Directly across from Auridan stood the statue of a plumed snake rearing up twice the height of a man, its mouth open in a silent hiss. Before the statue was a low table, and in front of it stood three men. The first was an old man robed in green. Next to him stood the sword-seller in an identical robe of dark blue. Then Auridan stiffened in shock. The third man was Lord Hervan.

"Your champion has arrived at last, Sympas," said the first man. He laughed unpleasantly, and his eyes never left Auridan. "Not a very prepossessing sight, is he?"

"Appearances are not everything, Kessas," the sword-seller replied calmly.

Kessas snorted. "It took you long enough to get him here."

Auridan stared at the two men in bewilderment. Beside him, Cyndal raised her head to study their surroundings. Auridan felt her shudder against him as her eyes fell on the statue; then she went rigid with shock. *"Hervan?"*

Hervan looked at her with a miserable expression. "I'm sorry, Cyndal! I didn't *know!*"

"Didn't know what?" Cyndal demanded. She sounded more like herself, and Auridan grinned.

"I didn't know what Kessas would ask! I . . . made a bargain, I thought it was the right thing, the only way to be *sure* . . ."

"What are you talking about, Hervan?" Cyndal said sharply.

"This," Hervan said. He looked away from her. "Your being here."

"What your step-cousin is trying to tell you is that either you or he will die tonight," said Kessas. Auridan made an involuntary gesture with his sword, and the old man gave him an unpleasant smile. "Precisely," he said.

"Hervan, *why?*" Cyndal said urgently.

Hervan raised his head. "Syledale. You know what it was like, after your uncle died! I wanted— I wanted to be sure nothing like that would ever happen again. There had to be an heir no one could question, but Chathalla hadn't shown the slightest sign, not once in over three years. So I bargained. I didn't know!"

"Enough," said Sympas sternly. "You made your agreement, and you must abide by it. By your own will, you are Kessas's champion."

"And I suppose you intend me to be yours," Auridan said.

"I chose you for that purpose, yes."

"What happens if I refuse?"

"If there is no contest, the color of the serpent

remains as it is, which is the green of Kessas," the sword-seller replied. "Since he is dominant, his will would prevail and the girl would be sacrificed."

Cyndal made a small noise and reached for the dagger at her belt. Auridan's eyes narrowed. "And if I agree?"

"The outcome of the contest determines the color of the serpent," Sympas said. "If Lord Hervan wins, Kessas remains dominant and the girl dies. But if you are the victor, the color of the serpent will change to blue, and you and the girl will go free."

"You leave me no choice," Auridan said.

"Then stop this chattering and let the contest begin," Kessas snarled.

Auridan raised his left hand and unfastened the clasp of his cloak. He let the soggy mass slide to the floor and stepped forward. Reluctantly, Hervan drew his sword and came to meet him. Auridan saw that Hervan's blade was a twin to his own, and his lips twisted. Not an identical twin, he thought; he would be willing to wager that the stones in the hilt of Hervan's sword were green, not blue.

Warily, Auridan circled his opponent. He had no idea how good a swordsman Hervan was, and still less what difference the two strange swords might make in the fight. Hervan was equally unwilling to close with him, but finally he could wait no longer. He stepped forward and swung.

Green and blue sparks flew as the weapons

touched, and Auridan felt his sword arm tingle. He forced himself to concentrate on fighting. Hervan was an excellent swordsman; Auridan could not afford to let himself be distracted. He parried a vicious thrust, and more sparks flew. They grew thicker and brighter with each blow, until the very air seemed to shine with green and blue light.

Finally, Hervan broke through Auridan's guard. Auridan twisted aside, but not quite in time. The point of Hervan's sword grazed his left shoulder. Auridan felt a painful jolt in his left arm from shoulder to fingertips. He ignored the pain, for Hervan's desperate attack had left an opening. With all his strength, Auridan brought his sword down across Hervan's, just above the guard. The force of the blow tore the weapon from Hervan's hand. Before he could recover it, Auridan's blade was at his throat.

Hervan stood motionless, staring at Auridan with wide eyes. Auridan hesitated, and heard the sword-seller's voice say, "You have won; now make an end."

Auridan shook his head. He stepped back, kicking Hervan's sword well out of reach, and lowered his own weapon. "If I have won, that is the end," he said. "There is no need for killing."

"You must!" Kessas's voice was frantic. "The power will not be bound unless the victory is sealed in blood!"

"I won't kill him," Auridan said stubbornly.

"Fool!" Kessas cried. "Kill him or we'll all die! Look there!"

Auridan looked up. The serpent statue was glowing. Blue and green light rippled up and down the carved plumes, the shimmering colors shifting crazily from one feather to another, and cracks were appearing in the stone. Kessas's face was a mask of terror. Then, with a loud grinding noise, a large chunk fell out of the nose of the statue. Another followed. "Run!" shouted the sword-seller.

Auridan ran. He heard Kessas shrieking curses behind him, but he did not look back. He saw the black barrier at the mouth of the cave vanish as Cyndal darted through it. An instant later, Auridan followed her, with Sympas right behind him. Auridan turned and pulled Hervan out just as the roof of the cave collapsed with a roar.

For a moment, they stood in the darkness outside, panting with exertion and coughing in the cloud of dust spewing from the mouth of the cave. The rain had subsided into a cold drizzle once more, which added to their discomfort. Sympas seemed the least affected; he stood staring almost wistfully back toward the cave. At last he looked up.

"The power of the serpent, for good or for ill, is broken, and I am free at last," he said to Auridan. "For that, my thanks."

"Thanks are well enough," Cyndal said with

irritation, "but I want an explanation. What has all this been about?"

The sword-seller smiled. "A fair question, though perhaps not fairly phrased. The feathered serpent that you saw in the cave was a . . . source of Power. In itself, it was neither of the Light nor of the Dark, but could serve either as its servants willed it.

"My brother and I were bound to the serpent long ago. We were intended to hold the serpent's Power for the Light, but over the years Kessas delved too deeply into the things of the Dark, and it swallowed him. Then he began searching for a way to bind the Power of the statue to himself alone.

"He found it in you." The sword-seller looked at Cyndal. "Your mother bore a trace of the old blood, and she passed it on to you. That and your beauty made you the perfect sacrifice, whose blood would bind the Power to Kessas. So Kessas made his bargain with your cousin: a son and heir in exchange for you."

"He didn't tell me what he was going to do!" Hervan said. "I wouldn't have agreed if I'd known."

"You did not ask," Sympas said sternly. Hervan looked down, and Sympas continued, "I learned of Kessas's actions too late to stop what he had set in motion. My only hope was to counter what he had done by choosing a champion of my own." His eyes met Auridan's, and he smiled. "I chose better than I knew."

"That was why you tried to give me the sword!" Auridan said.

"Yes. I was concerned when you insisted on paying, for it meant I had no hold on you to draw you here. So I sent you to Cyndal, hoping that you would become involved in her plans. In the end, it was as well that you were free to choose, for you could not otherwise have destroyed the serpent."

"I didn't—"

"The laws that governed the Power of the statue were very rigid. Blood sacrifice would bind its Power to Kessas; a contest to the death would bind its Power to the victor. You won the fight, but refused to kill your opponent. Neither Kessas nor I had won, and the conflicting Powers tore the statue apart. Had you taken the sword as I meant you to, I think you would not have been able to keep to your resolve."

Auridan looked at Hervan. The Dales lord looked cold and miserable and worried. Auridan still didn't like him much, but he was glad he had not been forced to kill the man.

"What about Chathalla?" Hervan asked urgently. "Will she be all right, now that . . ." He waved at the pile of rubble where the mouth of the cave had been.

"Your lady will suffer no hurt by this," Sympas assured him.

"You are luckier than you deserve, Hervan," Cyndal said.

"I know," Hervan said without looking at her.

"Then do not seek again to bend old Powers to your wishes," Sympas told him.

"I won't," Hervan assured him. Then he looked at Cyndal and said tentatively, "Will you still be going on to Norstead?"

"I think it would be best," Cyndal said gently. "If Auridan is still willing to guide me. But I will return before Chathalla has her child."

"Thank you," Hervan said.

The sword-seller looked at Auridan. "If you have no other questions for me, I must go."

"What about this?" Auridan said, holding out the short-sword.

"Keep it," Sympas said, and smiled. "You have paid for it twice over, once in coin and once in service."

"I'm not sure I want a sword that gives off blue sparks in a fight," Auridan said.

"The sword drew its Power from the statue; with the statue gone, you have no need to worry," Sympas assured him.

Auridan did not see how Sympas could be so positive, but he did not like to offend the man. He nodded and sheathed the sword, reminding himself mentally to clean it as soon as he was somewhere dry.

"Farewell, and again, my thanks." Sympas turned and started walking up the mountain.

"Wait! Where are you going?" Cyndal said.

The sword-seller looked back and smiled. "Home," he said, and this time when he walked away no one stopped him.

The Lorelei

THE TOUR BUS LURCHED DOWN to the end of the parking lot and expired in a cloud of blue smoke right in front of the ice-cream stand. Janet wondered whether the driver had planned it. Maybe he had an arrangement with the man who ran the ice-cream stand. Maybe he always stopped here when he was driving a busload of kids.

Mr. Norberg leaned forward and said something to the driver. Janet didn't bother trying to overhear; they were too far away, and her German wasn't that good anyway. Now he was talking to Mrs. Craig. Janet bet he was translating. Mrs. Craig's German was even worse than Janet's, but the school had had to have at least one female teacher along on the trip to chaperone the girls, and Mrs. Craig was the only one they could find who knew even a little German.

Janet saw Mrs. Craig nod, and Mr. Norberg stood up. "Everybody out!" he called. "Stay together and follow me, and don't wander off till I'm done with my speech. Mrs. Craig will bring up the rear, to make sure nobody gets mislaid. We can't afford to spend much time here if we want to get to Marksburg Castle yet today."

"Then why are we stopping at all?" Will Forney said from the seat behind Janet. His voice was loud enough to be heard for a couple of seats around him, but too low to carry to the front of the bus.

"Ice cream," Janet whispered back, and ducked her head to keep Mr. Norberg from seeing her expression.

"Everybody got that?" Mr. Norberg said. "All right, then, *raus.*"

There was some good-natured shoving as the bus emptied and a lot of milling around in the parking lot. Janet noted that Linda Sommers had taken advantage of the confusion to slip over to the ice-cream stand and buy one of the triple-chocolate bars. Linda was always doing things like that.

"Everybody out? All right; this way," Mr. Norberg said, and started off.

He led the way across the parking lot and around to the right of the little *Gasthaus*. Janet was rather proud of herself for thinking of it as a *Gasthaus,* rather than a hotel; it made her feel as if she wasn't just an ordinary tourist. She smiled to herself, and then she tripped on the curb and nearly ran into Dan Carpenter from behind. He gave her a look that made her feel twice as clumsy as she had actually been, but at least he didn't say anything.

"Watch out," said Heather Martin, who had come up beside Janet. "You nearly fell on me."

"I did not," Janet answered automatically. "And if I had fallen on anybody, it would have been Dan. You weren't even close."

"You missed me by an inch," Heather insisted. "Honestly, some people are so—"

"Shhh! Mr. Norberg's going to say something."

Heather craned her neck to see over Dan's head, and Janet nipped around the outside of the group to a place nearer the front. There was no point in arguing with Heather once she decided something; all you could do was get away from her until she found someone else to complain at.

"Watch your step here!" Mr. Norberg called. The stone footpath curved around behind the *Gasthaus,* then dropped into three wide, shallow steps and vanished altogether. Beyond was a large area of lumpy gray rock, with an iron railing on its far side. There were a few scrubby trees on the other side of the railing, but as Janet came closer she realized there was nothing beyond them but air.

"Can everybody hear me?" Mr. Norberg said. "Good. We're standing on the bedrock at the top of the Lorelei cliff. Those of you who've had my third-year German class will remember it from the poem by Heinrich Heine."

There were groans from the seniors, and some of the juniors looked nervously from them to Mr. Norberg and back. Sure enough, Mr. Norberg's next comment was, "Who wants to explain who the Lorelei is, for the benefit of the second-year students?"

"Nobody," whispered Rob Shonasai, and Janet smothered a giggle.

Despite Rob's comment, there were at least three hands raised. Mr. Norberg looked them over and shook his head. "I'd hoped that more of you would have better memories. Dan?"

"The Lorelei was a beautiful woman who sat on a cliff and sang when the boats went by on the Rhine River," Dan said. "The boatmen who heard her forgot what they were doing and crashed on the rocks." He sounded vaguely bored. Janet wondered why he had bothered to raise his hand. Maybe he'd just wanted to show off.

"Admirably succinct, though unromantic," Mr. Norberg said. "The Lorelei is, in fact, a German version of the Greek Sirens who gave Ulysses so much trouble. Ulysses got around them by plugging up his sailors' ears, but unfortunately that solution never occurred to the Germans."

"Why not?" Janet said, then immediately felt stupid because everyone turned to look at her. Dan Carpenter was practically sneering.

Mr. Norberg wasn't, though. "Probably because it wouldn't have done them any good. Look down at the river. See those two bends? They're close together, and the current is very strong. Furthermore, there used to be a lot of rocks in the water. Until they were dynamited early in this century, this part of the river was extremely dangerous."

"So the Lorelei is just something people made up to explain why they kept wrecking their boats here," Dan murmured, sounding interested at last.

"Phooey," said Heather. "I think the Lorelei is much more romantic."

Dan gave her a look. "You would."

Mr. Norberg let them take pictures, though he warned everyone several times to stay well behind the iron guard railing. Looking down the steep, rocky cliff, Janet could see why. Just looking made her dizzy.

"People still die here, you know," Lynnanne Gregory said beside her.

"What? What are you talking about?" Janet said, turning away from the drop with relief.

"I read about it in the guidebook this morning." Lynnanne dropped her voice to a thrilling whisper. "They jump off."

"That's not funny, Lynnanne." Janet stepped

back, letting someone else take her place beside the iron railing. "This place is creepy enough without bringing up stuff like that."

"I didn't say it was funny. But every year, two or three people—"

"I don't want to hear about it!" Before Lynnanne could continue, Janet shoved her way through the small group of students who were still waiting for a turn at the railing and went to join the larger group with Mr. Norberg. At least they were almost finished here; even if the castle at Marksburg had ghosts, it couldn't be as bad as the cliff.

When everyone was finished with their pictures, Mr. Norberg led them around the opposite side of the *Gasthaus*. On this side, someone had put up a statue of the Lorelei, made of gray-white stone. The sculptor thought the Lorelei was a tall, thin woman with long, wavy hair everywhere and a face that was sad and fierce and grim all at the same time. The statue made Janet shiver, and she gave it a wide berth.

Unfortunately, Peter Fletch noticed. "Hey, Janet, what's the matter? Scared of the witch?"

"No," Janet said. She didn't sound convincing even to herself.

"You don't have to be scared," Peter said in a tone of false consolation. "You're not a sailor. You're a girl."

Janet felt herself flushing, and she longed to make

a properly cutting remark, but her tongue was tied in knots. Then, from behind her, Beth Davidson said, "Don't be a sexist pig, Pete."

"I didn't say she was *just* a girl," Peter said, suddenly defensive. "I just said she *was* a girl, and she is."

"And you are pond scum," Beth said amiably. "And if we don't hurry, Linda's going to clean out the ice-cream stand before we get there. You want ice cream, or do you want to hang around arguing about who's insulting whom?"

Peter started to reply, thought better of it, and headed for the ice-cream stand, which was already surrounded by students from the tour. Beth shook her head. "Pond scum," she repeated. "You coming, Jan?"

"In a minute." Janet couldn't decide which would be worse, staying near the statue or joining the mob by the stand. Finally, she headed for the bus instead. If she hung around for a while, maybe she could grab a good seat when they got started again.

The bus driver and Mr. Norberg were holding a conference in German that was far beyond Janet's ability to follow. It involved much waving of arms and several emphatic phrases that Janet committed to memory in hopes that they might be swear words. She had a dictionary of German idioms that might shed some light on the question, now that she had some idea where to start looking.

Mr. Norberg turned away with a sigh and saw her. "Janet, would you fetch Mrs. Craig, please? I need to talk to her immediately."

Janet nodded. If she brought Mrs. Craig back, she'd probably find out what was going on, because Mr. Norberg would have to explain it in English. But if she had to guess, she'd bet there was something wrong with the bus.

She was right. The bus was dead, and within five minutes everyone knew it, though Mr. Norberg didn't officially announce that there was a problem until their twenty-minute break was over and they should have been getting on board again. It took another hour for the mechanic to arrive, and an hour after that before he admitted that he wouldn't have the parts to fix the engine until the following day. Mr. Norberg spent most of that time on the *Gasthaus* telephone, trying to persuade the tour company to send them another bus. The tour company refused, on the grounds that all their buses were busy.

This led to another flurry of conferences between Mr. Norberg, Mrs. Craig, the mechanic, the *Gasthaus* manager, and an Australian tourist with a rental car who was either very anxious to be helpful or very nosy, depending on whether you asked Mrs. Craig or Peter Fletch. Finally, Mr. Norberg called a conference

"Our bus isn't going to be fixed until tomorrow," Mr. Norberg told them. "We won't know until then how many stops we're going to have to skip or cut short in order to get back on schedule. Tonight, though, we're going to have to stay here."

"The Lorelei witch strikes again!" Will Forney said.

"Don't be stupid," Heather Martin told him. "The Lorelei didn't wreck things. She just sang."

"This *Gasthaus* doesn't have quite enough room for everybody," Mr. Norberg went on, "so I'm going to take some of the boys down to St. Goarshausen for the night. Eight of you will ride with Herr Schoengrum, the mechanic; and Mr. Colinwood has kindly offered to drive a few more down in his car. The rest of you will stay here with Mrs. Craig. Mike, Todd, Gordon—" He read off a list of names, and the boys went to collect their bags. A few people had questions; the rest, including Janet, drifted away to help unload bags or do some more exploring.

Janet crossed the parking lot and sat down on a rock. She wished that she were a boy; then she wouldn't have to stay in this creepy place. But if she were a boy, she probably wouldn't think it was creepy, or even if she were a girl like Lynnanne or Beth. She sighed. *It's only for one night,* she told herself. *Not so long.*

The boys who were going with Mr. Norberg loaded their bags onto the top of the mechanic's van; then a small mob of them crammed inside. Mr. Norberg and three others and the bus driver got in the car with the Australian tourist, and a few minutes later they had all left.

It was an hour later that Janet realized that one of the boys was missing.

She wasn't sure how she knew. She wasn't sure how long he had been gone. She wasn't even sure *which* of the boys was missing. It wasn't Will Forney or Rob Shonasai; they were standing by the back of the broken-down bus, squinting at the engine in the fading light and arguing with each other. Beth was there, too, because she thought engines were interesting, and Linda was sidling up on them because she thought Will was interesting and she didn't want Beth to get in ahead of her. Rich Conway was slouching against the corner of the ice-cream stand. Peter Fletch was nowhere in sight, but only a few minutes earlier Janet had seen him slip around the far corner of the *Gasthaus,* so it couldn't be him, either.

Carefully, Janet counted over in her mind all the boys who had gone with Mr. Norberg. Eight in the mechanic's van, and three in the car with Mr. Norberg and the Australian tourist who'd offered to help. Eleven boys. If Will and Rob and Rich and Peter were the only ones who were supposed to be staying with Mrs. Craig, there should have been twelve who'd left with Mr. Norberg. But there had only been eleven.

If she could only remember the names of everyone

who'd left, she'd know who was missing now. But she hadn't been paying close enough attention when Mr. Norberg rattled off his list.

Mrs. Craig appeared suddenly in the door of the *Gasthaus,* calling and waving. Dinner must be ready. Janet thought briefly about telling her someone was gone, then shook her head. Mrs. Craig would just say Janet must have miscounted.

Maybe she had. Maybe there had been twelve boys with Mr. Norberg. Maybe she was worrying about nothing. Janet sighed as she followed the others into the *Gasthaus.* Maybe she was wrong, but she couldn't quite convince herself. If only Susan could have come on this trip, too . . . But Susan was back in Wilmette, Illinois, and Janet didn't know the rest of the girls well enough to talk to. Not about anything important, anyway.

The problem preoccupied her through the first half of dinner, so much that she even ate a bite of the dubious-looking shredded vegetables before she realized what she was doing. She swallowed quickly and took a gulp of her orange drink to wash the taste away, hoping no one would notice. From then on, Janet tried to pay more attention to eating and the table talk. She even managed to convince herself that she had no reason to be worried. At least, she thought she had convinced herself of that, until Beth grabbed her arm as she was getting up from the table and said, "Wait a minute, Jan. I want to talk to you."

"What about?" Janet said warily.

"Which half of the room you want; whether you read in bed with a flashlight; how early you set your alarm. Mrs. Craig's shuffled all the room assignments around; the two of us are sharing tonight."

"Oh. Sure." Janet sank back down into her chair. She had been rooming with Lynnanne, who had twice as many bags as anyone else on the trip and who would have changed clothes four times a day if she could have gotten away with it. Janet wondered what it would be like to room with Beth, who argued about car engines with the boys and who seemed perfectly happy to wear the same jeans and Kmart sweater for days at a time.

The other girls drifted away from the table. Beth glanced around the neat little dining room and leaned forward. "All right, Jan, what's the matter with you?" she said bluntly.

"I— Nothing," Janet said weakly.

"Baloney. Something has you spooked. I can tell. Unless you're still upset about this afternoon?"

"You mean the business with Peter? No. But I can't explain. It'll just sound weird and stupid."

"S'all right; you've warned me," Beth said. "So what is it?"

"I think somebody's missing," Janet said, and launched into a more detailed explanation before Beth could object that that was ridiculous. It felt wonderful to tell someone. Beth listened intently, and when Janet finished she sat frowning at the tabletop. "Do you think we should tell Mrs. Craig?" Janet asked doubtfully after a minute. "Do you think she'll believe us?"

"I don't know," Beth said. She was still frowning. "I don't know if I believe it. I mean, you aren't even sure yourself. And Mr. Norberg and Mrs. Craig are pretty careful about counting heads. They wouldn't just mislay somebody."

"I know, I know," Janet said. "But still . . ."

"And where would your missing person have gotten to?" Beth went on remorselessly. "Somebody would have noticed if he'd fallen off the cliff; there are boats and tourists and cars on the road all day."

"So maybe I'm crazy." Janet stared past Beth at the darkness outside the *Gasthaus* windows and shivered. "This place is weird. Maybe the pine trees and the echo and the mountains and everything are making me crazy."

"Spruce. They're spruce trees, not pine."

Janet made an exasperated noise. "I don't care what they are! Haven't you been listening?"

"Mmmm-hmmmm. Tell you what—let's go look around outside. Maybe we'll find something."

Janet nodded, and together they went out. The sun had set, but a bright half-moon was already well up in the sky. The bus was a shadowy lump on the far side of the parking lot, with the sharply pointed silhouettes of the evergreens behind it. "I bet the bus is locked up," Janet said.

"If we don't look, we'll never know," Beth replied.

The bus door was locked, but the baggage compartments underneath were open. Beth dug a flashlight out of the little green backpack she carried instead of a purse and swept its beam into every corner. "Empty," she said at last in tones of great satisfaction.

"So?" Janet said.

"So if somebody's missing, they'll find out when they sort out the luggage. So you can quit worrying."

"I suppose— What's that?"

"What's what?" Beth said. "I don't hear anything."

"Shhh," Janet hissed. Beth shrugged, but she didn't say anything else. Janet strained her ears to catch the sound she had heard. For a long moment, there were only the noises from the *Gasthaus* windows: the clatter of dishes being cleared, Lynnanne and Maggie yelling about something in one of the upstairs rooms, the shouts of the boys clowning around as they carried their bags up to their rooms. Then she heard it again. "I think it's music."

"Music?"

"Singing." Suddenly Janet felt very frightened. "Come on," she said, and began to run.

The beam of Beth's flashlight followed her for a moment, then cut off abruptly. Janet ran around the corner of the *Gasthaus,* past the ghostly white stone of the Lorelei statue and on toward the cliff's edge.

The singing was growing—not louder, but easier to hear. She no longer had to strain to pick out the soft, sweet music from among the shouts and laughter leaking out of the *Gasthaus* and the noise of her own breathing.

The dirt footpath was slanted and uneven. Janet stumbled and had to slow down. And then there was rock under her feet, rough and lumpy, and she had reached the clear area at the cliff's edge. The sound of the singing was all around her, but the clearing was empty. Through the gap in the trees at the far side, she could see the lights of St. Goarshausen below, along the river's edge. The Rhine itself was a broad, dark belt with just a glimmer of silver along the far shore where the moonlight was beginning to touch it.

The glimmer spread and grew brighter, and Janet blinked. Suddenly there was a woman leaning against the iron railing that was supposed to keep tourists from falling down the cliff. Her head was thrown back, and her hair hung loose and pale, almost to her feet. She wore a long, loose tunic that came down past her knees and underneath it a full skirt that covered her feet. Her skin glowed faintly, white and cold, like the glitter of the moonlight on the Rhine. She was singing.

"Stop that!" Janet shouted.

The singing stopped, and there was an eerie silence, sudden and complete. There was no noise from the traffic on the riverside highway, no rustling of the wind in the trees, no faintest sound of shouts and giggles from the *Gasthaus* a few hundred yards away. Janet could hear nothing but the sound of her own breathing.

The woman lowered her head and seemed to see Janet for the first time. The expression on her face made Janet feel as if her jeans were torn, her sweater stretched out of shape, and her hair limp and greasy.

Janet clenched her teeth together, the way she did when Lynnanne was being snide, and took a step forward. "You're the Lorelei, aren't you?"

"Clever child," said the woman. "Yes."

"Where is he?" Janet said fiercely.

"Where is who?" said the Lorelei. Her lips moved without showing her teeth, and the motions didn't seem to fit her words. It was like watching a foreign movie with the sound dubbed in English. With a slight sense of shock, Janet realized that the Lorelei was speaking German, but Janet was hearing her in English.

"The boy who disappeared this afternoon," Janet said. "You've got him, haven't you? Where is he?"

"Ah. Him." A flicker of expression crossed the Lorelei's face, but it was gone before Janet could tell what it was. "He's one of the stubborn ones." She looked at Janet with a trace of interest. "I suppose you, too, are stubborn, or you would not have heard my song."

Janet wondered what was taking Beth so long to catch up. She felt cold and scared, and all she could do about it was to demand for a third time, "Where is he?"

The Lorelei smiled, and her teeth were dark and pointed. She gestured toward the cliff's edge.

Janet swallowed hard and forced her legs to carry her across the rough rock. She gave the Lorelei a wide berth and caught hold of the iron railing farther along. Taking a deep breath, she clenched her hands around the rail and leaned over to look down the cliff.

At first she could see little. The moon was behind her, illuminating the clearing and the ragged gray tops of the rocks in front of her, but then the cliff sloped steeply down into shadow. It was not a sheer drop, and lower down a forest of full-grown trees hid the rocks and soil. Even near the top, where Janet stood, there were small, scrubby trees clinging to cracks and hollows in the rock. Then her eyes began to adjust, and she saw that one of the dark places was not a hollow at all.

He was pressed flat against the rock; all Janet could see was his back and the top of his head and the arm he had flung sideways to grab at the roots of a bush. She could hear him panting in great gasps, as if he had run too far, too fast. He was only about twenty feet below her, but it might as well have been a mile.

"Hey!" Janet called, unable to think of anything else. "Hey, are you all right?"

The boy on the rocks raised his head and stared

blindly upward. "Who's that?" he said. "You don't sound like— Who is it?"

"Dan?" Janet said incredulously. "Dan Carpenter?" Hearing herself, she realized that deep down inside she hadn't really believed any of this until now—not the missing boy, nor the odd quiet of the air, and most especially not the Lorelei witch leaning against the iron rail a few feet away and watching with enigmatic eyes.

"Who is it?" Dan said again, and this time his voice didn't sound quite as strained as before.

"It's me, Jan Laine. I came out looking for . . ." Janet let the sentence trail off, unable to explain in any convincing manner just how she happened to be there. Especially not to Dan.

"Has she gone, then?" Dan demanded.

Before Janet could answer, the Lorelei began to sing again. Her voice was low and soft and sweet, but it had the penetrating quality of Holly Fitzgerald's flute when she was trying to hit the top note loudly and missing. The words of the song seemed to flow together and twine around each other, and Janet could not catch any of them clearly. Underneath the words, behind the music, Janet could hear something strong and wild and fearful, but it could not touch her. The song and the dangerous underside of the song streamed past Janet and down the cliffside.

Dan's face twisted as the Lorelei's singing reached

him. He began scrambling up the rocky cliff toward Janet, moving with reckless speed. Janet could see dark scratches on his face and hands, and she was terrified that at any moment he would slip. She crouched beside the railing, holding her breath and wishing she had a rope or a belt or anything she could throw down to Dan. She didn't think she could stand watching him roll and slip and crash down the side of the cliff, even if she didn't like him much. "Stop it!" she screamed at the Lorelei.

The Lorelei did not seem to hear; her eyes and all her attention were on Dan. Her expression was not emotionless anymore; there was a fierce pleasure in it, and an eager anticipation. Janet stood up and started toward the creature. She didn't know what she was going to do, but she had to make the Lorelei stop singing.

The Lorelei stopped. Janet was completely taken aback for a moment; then she turned and saw Dan climbing under the guardrail onto the cliff top. His shirt was torn, and Janet could see the mud stains on his jeans even in the moonlight. She let out a breath of relief. Behind her, the Lorelei laughed.

Janet looked back at the Lorelei. The witch smiled her pointed smile; then her figure shimmered and spread like moonlight on the river below. An instant later, she was gone.

Janet stared. Finally she drew a deep breath.

"Well," she said in a shaky voice, "well, that's good, anyway."

"She's just playing cat-and-mouse," Dan said. "She's been playing it with me for—for quite a while, I think."

"Then let's get out of here before she comes back," Janet said, and started for the *Gasthaus*.

"It won't do any good," Dan said, without moving. "Do you think I haven't tried?"

"What do you mean?"

"I told you, she's playing. She lets me get three or four steps, and then the singing starts again. Once she let me get all the way to the end of the path before she hauled me back."

"I can go, though. I can get Mrs. Craig." Janet knew, even as she said it, that this would do no good at all, even if she could get away from the charmed cliff top, even if she could think up a story Mrs. Craig would believe. The Lorelei had slipped and let Janet through into this strange, silent world, but she would not slip twice. If Janet left now, she would not be able to get back until the Lorelei's games were over, any more than Beth had been able to follow Janet into the Lorelei's world.

"You know better," Dan said.

"You suggest something, then!" Janet said, but as she spoke the singing started again.

This time the song came from the foot of the cliff.

Dan made a gasping noise and lurched across the rock toward the guardrail. Janet stood motionless for a moment, in a frozen rage at the Lorelei witch, who had found this new game to play when the rocks in the river were blown up and her songs could no longer lure boatmen to crash on them. Like a German Siren, Mr. Norberg had said . . .

Dan had almost reached the railing. Janet ran forward and jumped onto his back. He staggered and they fell sideways together. Janet clapped her hands over his ears and clung tightly. Dan seemed dazed, unable to help or hinder.

Suddenly, the Lorelei's song changed, becoming softer and more plaintive. It tugged at Janet, and she became aware of how tired she was and of all the places where she had been bruised when she fell. She wanted to go back to the *Gasthaus* and relax in the light and warmth, to forget about all this unpleasantness and become absorbed in her embroidery . . .

Embroidery? "I don't sew," Janet said loudly. "And even if I did, I wouldn't let you have anybody just because I wanted to be comfortable for a few minutes. Maybe that's what people did three hundred years ago, but not anymore!"

The singing faltered, then changed again. This time it whispered promises. Janet saw herself at the center of a group of boys, all begging for dates. Even Peter Fletch, who was apologizing for ever having teased her about anything. The girls were there and liked her, too, and all of it could happen if she only let go of this one boy . . .

"I hate being the center of attention, and you can't have him!" Janet snarled.

The Lorelei's song changed key in a mournful run of notes and grew louder and more threatening. Janet was foolish to be so stubborn. She couldn't win, and in the end she would be blamed. Or perhaps the Lorelei would take her instead of Dan. She would fall down that dizzying slope and break to pieces on the rocks below, like the boats and the boatmen.

Janet took her left hand off of Dan's ear and clapped it against her own. The sick fear receded a little, but not enough . . . and Dan twisted and pulled away. Her other hand slipped. Dan twisted again and threw her off, then hoisted himself to his feet and started for the edge of the slope again.

Janet scrambled after him. The Lorelei's song rang in her ears, whispering that he would pull her over the cliff's edge with him if she tried to stop him again. Janet gritted her teeth and flung herself forward. She reached Dan just as he came to the guardrail, and slapped her hands over his ears. He stopped, staring at her, while the Lorelei sang fear and failure with renewed intensity.

She wasn't going to make it. She knew she wasn't, even without the growing triumph she could hear in the Lorelei's voice. In another minute, she would have to let go of Dan's ears to cover her own, she could feel it. She bit her lip, trying to distract herself, but it didn't help. And then Dan raised his hands and covered her ears.

The song diminished to a bearable level at once. Janet sighed in relief. Just in time, she remembered not to take her own hands away from Dan's ears. That really would be stupid. On the other hand, how long could they stand here like this? If only Beth would come, or Mrs. Craig, or somebody . . . But if they did, what would they think when they found her standing with Dan in the moonlight, each holding on to the other's ears? The image was too much, and she began to giggle. Dan looked down, startled, and the giggle turned into a laugh at the expression on his face. In another moment, Dan was laughing, too.

As they laughed, the remaining pressure on Janet vanished, and when she stopped chuckling she realized that the Lorelei's song had ceased. After a moment's hesitation, she slowly lowered her hands. Dan shivered, then did the same.

"Thanks," he said to Janet. He looked as if he would have liked to say more, but wasn't quite sure what.

Janet nodded, accepting both the spoken and the unspoken thought. "Thanks to you, too. She was starting to get to me."

"I finally figured that out," Dan said. "I don't know why it took me so long. I— Heads up!"

Janet turned. The Lorelei was standing a few feet

farther down the cliff's edge, watching them, her face an expressionless mask. Hastily, Janet reached for Dan's ears again, but the Lorelei shook her head.

"That is unnecessary now," the Lorelei said. "You have won." She gave Janet a long, measuring look. "I have never been defeated by ones as young as you before. You have great strength, girl."

Janet found herself unwilling to say anything to the Lorelei, so she settled for a shrug.

The Lorelei's gaze moved to Dan, and she smiled coldly. "You have learned something, I think. Do not forget it." She held Dan's eyes briefly, then looked back at Janet. "Go, then, the pair of you."

Dan started toward the footpath at once, and Janet was not far behind him. As they crossed from the moon-made silver of the bare rock to the packed dirt of the footpath, the world seemed to tilt briefly and resettle itself in a different shape. They heard the sound of running feet in front of them. "Hey, look out!" Janet said.

"I'm looking, I'm looking." Beth panted as she came to a halt. "I see you found somebody."

"It's a good thing for me that she did," Dan said.

"Well, you were right here, weren't you?" Beth said indignantly. "I wasn't that far behind. Boy, you can really run, Jan. I thought I'd lost you for a minute."

"You did," Janet said. She snuck a quick look back over her shoulder. The Lorelei was gone.

"Oh?" Beth looked from Janet to Dan, noting Dan's torn shirt and muddy jeans. "I smell a tall tale. Come sit in the parking lot and tell me, and then we'll figure out what to say to Mrs. Craig." She flicked her flashlight on, and the three of them started back toward the *Gasthaus*.

Stronger Than Time

THE KEEP ROSE HIGH above the ring of brush and briars choking the once-clear lawn around its base. Even when the sun was high, the tower's shadow lay cold and dark on the twisted mass of thorns, and at dusk it stretched like a gnarled black finger across the forest and up the mountainside. Arven hated walking through that somber dimness, though it was the shortest way home. Whenever he could, he swung wide around the far side of the keep to stay clear of its shadow. Most people avoided the keep altogether, but Arven found its sunlit face fascinating. The light colored the stone according to the time of day and the shifting of the seasons, now milk white and shining, now tinged with autumn gold or rosy with reflected sunset, now a grim winter gray. The shadowed side was always black and ominous.

Once, when he was a young man and foolish (he had thought himself brave then, of course), Arven had dressed in his soft wool breeches and the fine linen shirt his mother had embroidered for him and gone to the very edge of the briars. He had searched all along the sunlit side of the keep for an opening, a path, a place where the briars grew less thickly, but he had found nothing. Reluctantly, he had circled to the shadowed side. Looking back toward the light he had just quitted, he had seen white bones dangling inside the hedge, invisible from any other angle: human bones entwined with briars. There were more bones among the shadows, bones that shivered in the wind, and leaned toward him, frightening him until he ran away. He had never told anyone about it, not even Una, but he still had nightmares in which weather-bleached bones hung swaying in the wind. Ever since, he had avoided the shadow of the keep if he could.

Sometimes, however, he miscalculated the time it would take to fell and trim a tree, and then he had to take the short way or else arrive home long after the sun was down. He felt like a fool, hurrying through the shadows, glancing up now and again at the keep looming above him, and when he reached his cottage he was always in a bad temper. So he was not in the best of humors when, one autumn evening after such a trip, he found a young man in a voluminous cloak and a wide-brimmed hat, sitting on his doorstep in the gray dusk, waiting.

"Who are you?" Arven growled, hefting his ax to show that his white hair was evidence of mere age and not infirmity.

"A traveler," the man said softly without moving. His voice was tired, bone tired, and Arven wondered suddenly whether he was older than he appeared. Twilight could be more than kind to a man or woman approaching middle age; Arven had known those who could pass, at twilight, for ten or fifteen fewer years than what the midwife attested to.

"Why are you here?" Arven demanded. "The road to Prenshow is six miles to the east. There's nothing to bring a traveler up on this mountain."

"Except the keep," said the man in the same soft tone.

Arven took an involuntary step backward, raising his ax as if to ward off a threat. "I have nothing to do with the keep. Go back where you came from. Leave honest men to their work and the keep to crumble."

The man climbed slowly to his feet. "Please," he said, his voice full of desperation. "Please, listen to me. Don't send me away. You're the only one left."

No, I was mistaken, Arven thought. *He's no more than twenty, whatever the shadows hint. Such intensity belongs only to the young.* "What do you mean?"

"No one else will talk about the keep. I need—I need to know more about it. You live on the mountain; the keep is less than half a mile away. Surely you can tell me something."

"I can only tell you to stay away from it, lad." Arven set his ax against the wall and looked at the youth, who was now a gray blur in the deepening shadows. "It's a cursed place."

"I know." The words were almost too faint to catch, even in the evening stillness. "I've . . . studied the subject. Someone has to break the curse, or it will go on and on and . . . Tell me about the keep. Please. You're the only one who might help me."

Arven shook his head. "I won't help you kill yourself. Didn't your studies teach you about the men who've died up there? The briars are full of bones. Don't add yours to the collection."

The youth raised his chin. "They all went alone, didn't they? Alone, and in daylight, and so the thorns killed them. I know better than that."

"You want to go up to the keep at *night?*" A chill ran down Arven's spine, and he stared into the darkness, willing his eyes to penetrate it and show him the expression on the other's face.

"At night, with you. It's the only way left to break the curse."

"You're mad." But something stirred within Arven, a longing for adventure he had thought buried with Una and the worn-out rags of the embroidered linen shirt he had worn on their wedding day. The image of the keep, shining golden in the autumn sun, rose temptingly in his mind. He shook his head to drive away the memories and pushed open the door of his cottage.

"Wait!" said the stranger. "I shouldn't have said that, I know, but at least let me explain."

Arven hesitated. There was no harm in listening, and perhaps he could talk the young fool out of his suicidal resolve. "Very well. Come in."

The young man held back. "I'd rather talk here."

"Indoors, or not at all," Arven growled, regretting his momentary sympathy. "I'm an old man, and I want my dinner and a fire and something warm to drink."

"An old man?" The other's voice was startled, and not a little dismayed. "You can't be! It didn't take that long—" He stepped forward and peered at Arven, and the outline of his shoulders sagged. "I've been a fool. I won't trouble you further, sir."

"My name is Arven." Now that the younger man was turning to go, he felt a perverse desire to keep him there. "It's a long walk down the mountain. Come in and share my meal, and tell me your story. I like a good tale."

"I wouldn't call it a good one," the young man said, but he turned back and followed Arven into the cottage.

Inside, he stood uneasily beside the door while

Arven lit the fire and got out the cider and some bread and cheese. Una had always had something warm ready when Arven came in from the mountain, a savory stew or thick soup when times were good, a vegetable pottage when things were lean, but since her death he had grown accustomed to a small, simple meal of an evening. The young man did not appear to notice or care until Arven set a second mug of warm cider rather too emphatically on the table and said, "Your story, scholar?"

The young man shivered like a sleepwalker awakened abruptly from his dreams. "I'm not a scholar."

"Then what are you?"

The man looked away. "Nothing, now. Once I was a prince."

That explained the world-weariness in his voice, Arven thought. He'd been raised to rule and then lost all chance of doing so before he'd even begun. Probably not long ago, either, or the boy would have begun to forget his despair and plan for a new life, instead of making foolish gestures like attempting the keep. Arven wondered whether it had been war or revolution that had cost the young prince his kingdom. In these perilous times, it could have been either; the result was the same.

"Sit down, then, Your Highness, and tell me your tale," Arven said in a gentler tone.

"My tale isn't important. It's the keep—"

"The keep's tale, then," Arven interrupted with a trace of impatience.

The prince only nodded, as if Arven's irritability could not touch him. "It's not so much the story of the keep as of the counts who lived there. They were stubborn men, all of them, and none so stubborn as the last. Well, it takes a stubborn man to insult a witch-woman—even if he was unaware, as some have claimed—and then refuse to apologize for the offense."

Without conscious thought, Arven's fingers curled into the sign against evil. "The count did that? No wonder the keep is cursed!"

The prince flinched. "Not the keep, but what is within it."

"What?" Arven frowned and rubbed the back of his neck. Trust a nobleman to make hash of things instead of telling a simple, straightforward tale. "Go on."

"You see, the count's meeting with the witch-woman occurred at his daughter's christening, and the infant suffered as much or more than the father from the witch-woman's spell of revenge. Before the assembled guests, the witch declared that the girl would be the last of the count's line, for he would get no more children and his daughter would die of the pricking of a spindle before she turned sixteen. When the guards ran up, the witch laughed at them and vanished before they could lay hands on her.

"The count made fun of the curse at first, until he found that half of it at least was true. His daughter was the only child he would ever have. Then he raged like a wild man, but it did him no good. So he became wary of the second half of the curse, more because he did not wish his line to end than out of love for the girl.

"He was too stubborn to take her away, where the witch's power might not have reached. For seven generations, his father's fathers had lived in the keep, and he would not be driven away from it, nor allow his daughter to be raised anywhere else. Instead, he swore to defeat the curse on his own ground. He ordered every spindle in the castle burnt and banished spinners and weavers from his lands. Then he forbade his daughter to wander more than a bow shot from the outer wall. He thought that he had beaten the witch, for how could his daughter die of the pricking of a spindle in a keep where there were none?

"The count's lady wife was not so sanguine. She knew something of magic, and she doubted that the count's precautions would save her child. So she set herself to unravel the doom the witch had woven, pitting her love for her daughter against the witch-woman's spite."

"Love against death," Arven murmured.

"What was that?" the prince asked, plainly startled.

"It's something my wife used to say," Arven answered. His eyes prickled and he looked away, half out of embarrassment at being so openly sentimental, half out of a desire to cherish Una's memory in private.

"Oh?" The prince's voice prodded gently.

"She said that time and death are the greatest enemies all of us must face, and the only weapon stronger than they are is love." Arven thought of the grave behind the cottage, with its carpet of daisies and the awkward wooden marker he had made himself. He had always meant to have the stonemason carve a proper headstone, but he had never done it. Wood and flowers were better, somehow. Una would have laughed at the crooked marker, and hugged him, and insisted on keeping it because he had made it for her, and the flowers—she had loved flowers. The shadows by the wall wavered and blurred, and Arven rubbed the back of his hand across his eyes. Love might be stronger than death or time, but it had won him neither peace nor acceptance, even after five long years.

"Your wife was a wise woman," the prince said softly.

"Yes." Arven did not trust his voice for more than the one short word. The prince seemed to understand, for he went on with his story without waiting for Arven to ask.

"The countess was not skilled enough to undo the witch's curse completely, but she found a way to alter it. Instead of death, the prick of the spindle would cast her daughter into an enchanted sleep, never changing. The witch's curse would turn outward, protecting the girl for one hundred years by killing anyone who sought to enter her resting place. One hundred years to the day after the onset of the spell, a man would come, a prince or knight of great nobility, who could pass through the magical barriers without harm. His kiss would break the spell forever, and the girl would awake as if she had slept but a single night instead of a hundred years."

"And meanwhile men would die trying to get to her," Arven said, thinking of bones among briars. "It was a cruel thing to do."

"I doubt that the countess was thinking of anything but her daughter," the prince said uncomfortably.

"Nobles seldom think beyond their own concerns," Arven said. The prince looked down. Arven took pity on him, and added, "Well, it's a fault that's common enough in poor folk, too. Go on."

"There isn't much more to the story," the prince said. "Somehow, on the eve of her sixteenth birthday, the girl found a spindle and pricked her finger, setting the curse in motion. That was over a hundred years ago, and ever since, men have been dying in the attempt to break it."

"*Over* a hundred years? You said the curse would last a hundred years to the day."

"That's why I need your help." The prince leaned forward earnestly. "The curse was only supposed to last for a hundred years, but the countess wasn't as skilled in magic as she thought she was, and mixing spells is a delicate business. She was too specific about the means of breaking the curse, and now there is no way I can do it alone."

"Too specific?"

"She tied the ending of the curse to a precise day and the coming of a particular man. It would have worked well enough, if the right prince had been a steadier sort, but he was . . . impetuous." The prince looked down once more. "He arrived a day too soon, and died in the thorns."

"And thus the curse goes on." *The young are so impetuous,* Arven thought, *and it costs them so much.* "How do you know all this?"

"He was . . . a member of my family," the prince replied.

"Ah. And you feel you should put his error right?"

"I must." The prince raised his head, and even in the flickering firelight, naked longing was plain upon his face. "No one else can, and if the curse is not broken, more men will die and the countess's daughter will remain trapped in the spell, neither dead nor alive, while the castle crumbles around her."

"I thought the girl would come into it somewhere," Arven muttered, but the image touched him nonetheless. He and Una had never had a child, though they had wanted one. Sixteen—she would have been full of life and yearning for things she could not name.

He had known children cut off at such an age by disease or accident, and he had grieved with their parents over the tragedy of their loss, but now even the cruelest of those deaths seemed clean and almost right compared to this unnatural suspension. He shuddered and took a long pull at his mug. The cider had gone cold. "How do you hope to break the curse, if the right time and the right man both have come and gone?"

"I've studied this spell for a long time," the prince replied. "Two men can succeed where one must fail."

"How?" Arven insisted.

"The curse is really two spells muddled together. A single man, if he knew enough of magic, might hold it back for a few hours, but he couldn't clear a path through the briars at the same time. Sooner or later, his spell would falter and the thorns would kill him. With two men—"

"One can work the spell and the other can clear the path," Arven finished. He gave the prince a long, steady look. "You didn't really come looking for me to get information about the keep."

"No." The prince returned the look, unashamed. "But you wouldn't have listened if I'd begun by saying I wanted you to help me get inside."

"True enough." Arven considered. "Why at night?"

"I can only work the spell then."

Arven glanced sharply at the prince's face. He knew the sound of a half-truth, and that had been one. Still, there had been truth in it, and if the prince had additional reasons for choosing night over day, they could only strengthen his argument. Arven realized with wry humor that it did not matter any longer. He had made up his mind; all that remained was to nerve himself to act. That being so, hesitation would be a meaningless waste of time. He looked down and saw with surprise that his plate was empty; he had finished the bread and cheese without noticing, as they talked. He drained his mug and set it aside, then rose. "We'd best be on our way. Half a mile is a far distance, in the dark and uphill."

The prince's eyes widened. He stared at Arven for a long moment, then bowed his head. "Thank you," he said, and though the words were soft, they held a world of meaning and intensity. Again Arven wondered why this was so important to the younger man, but it made no real difference now. Whether the prince was trying to make up for the loss of his kingdom, or had become infatuated with the sleeping girl of his imagination, or truly wanted to repair the harm his unnamed uncle or cousin had done, Arven had agreed to help him.

"You take the lantern," Arven said, turning to lift it down from the peg beside the door.

"No," the prince said. As Arven looked back

in surprise, he added a little too quickly, "I need to . . . prepare my mind while we walk. For the spell."

"Thinking won't keep you from a fall," Arven said, irritated. "There's no moon tonight."

The prince only looked at him. After a moment, Arven gave up. He took the lantern down, filled and lit it, and carried it outside himself. He was half-inclined to tell the young prince to go on alone, but each time the words rose in his mouth he bit them back. He shifted the lantern to his left hand and picked up his ax, then glanced back toward the door. The prince was standing on the step.

Arven jerked his head to indicate the direction of the keep, then turned and set off without waiting to see whether the prince followed him or not. If the prince wanted a share of the lantern light, let him hurry; if not, it would only be justice if he tripped and rolled halfway down the mountain in the dark.

Thirty feet from the cottage, with the familiar breeze teasing the first fallen leaves and whispering among the beeches and the spruce, Arven's annoyance began to fade. It was not the prince's fault that he was young, nor that he was noble-born and therefore almost certainly unaware of the perils of a mountain forest at night. Arven paused and looked back, intending to wait or even go back a little way if necessary.

The prince was right behind him, a dim, indistinct

figure against the darker shapes of the trees. Arven blinked in surprise, and his opinion of the young man rose. Prince or not, he could move like a cat in the woods. Arven nodded in recognition and acceptance of the other man's skill, and turned back to the trail. He was annoyed at having been inveigled into misjudging the prince, but at the same time he was grateful not to have to play the shepherd for an untutored companion.

The walk up to the keep seemed to take longer than usual. The prince stayed a few steps behind, moving so quietly that Arven glanced back more than once to assure himself that his companion was still there. Mindful of the prince's comment about preparation, Arven did not try to speak to him.

At the edge of the briars, Arven halted. Though the keep was all but invisible in the darkness, he could feel its presence, a massive pile of stone almost indistinguishable from the mountain peaks, save that it was nearer and more menacing. "What now?" he asked as the prince came up beside him.

"Put out the light."

With more than a little misgiving, Arven did so. In the dim starlight, the briars reminded him of a tangle of sleeping snakes. Frowning, he untied the thongs and stripped the leather cover from his ax, feeling foolish because he had not done so before he put out the light. A breath of wind went past, not strong enough to ripple the prince's cloak but more than enough to remind Arven of the clammy fear-sweat on the back of his neck. *I'm too old for this,* he thought.

"Hold out your ax," the prince said.

Again, Arven did as he was told. The prince extended his hands, one on either side of the blade, not quite touching the steel. He murmured something, and a crackle of blue lightning sprang from his hands and ran in a net of thin, bright, crooked lines across the ax blade.

Arven jumped backward, dropping the ax. The light vanished, leaving a blinding afterimage that hid the ax, the briars, and the prince completely. Arven muttered a curse and rubbed at his eyes. When the dazzle began to clear, he bent and felt carefully across the ground for his ax. When he found it, he picked it up and slid a slow finger along the flat of the ax head toward the cutting edge, brushing off leaves and checking for nicks. Only when he was sure the ax was in good order did he say, "Your Highness?"

"I'm sorry," the prince's voice said out of the night. "I should have warned you."

"Yes."

"It will help with the briars."

"It had better." Arven wiped one hand down his side, then transferred the ax to it and wiped the other. "What else do you have to do?"

"I will restrain the thorns so that they will not harm you while you cut a path through them. I must warn you; I can only affect a small area. Beyond that, the briars will remain . . . active. The sight may be disturbing."

"This whole venture is disturbing," grumbled Arven. "Very well, I'm warned."

"One other thing: do not look back until you reach the castle gate. Your concentration is as important as mine; if you are distracted, we may both be lost."

"You're a cheerful one." Arven paused. "Are you sure you want to do this? I'm an old man . . ." *And you are young, with a long life, perhaps, if you leave this lunacy undone,* he thought, but did not say, because it was the same advice his elders had given him when he was young. The prince would probably pay as much attention to it as Arven had, which was none at all.

"You're the only one who would come with me," the prince said, misinterpreting Arven's question and confirming his opinion at the same time.

"You've about as much tact as you have sense," Arven said under his breath. He twisted the ax handle between his hands, feeling the smooth wood slide against his palms, and his fear melted away. He had worked these woods all his life; he knew the moods of the mountain in all times and seasons, and the moods of the keep as well; he had cut every kind of tree and cleared every kind of brush the forest had to offer, over and over. This was no different, really. He turned to face the briars and said over his shoulder, "Tell me when you are ready."

"Go," said the prince's voice softly, and Arven swung his ax high, stepped forward, and brought it down in a whistling arc to land with a dull, unerring thump an inch above the base of the first briar.

The stems were old and tough, and as thick as Arven's forearm. He struck again and again, and then his muscles caught the familiar rhythm of the work. A wind rose as he hacked and chopped and tossed aside. A corner of his mind listened intently for the warning creak of a tree about to fall in his direction, but otherwise he ignored the growing tempest.

All around, the briars shifted and began to thrash as the wind ripped their ends from their customary tangle to strike at air, straining against their roots. Where Arven stood, and for thrice the length of his ax in all directions around him, the air was calm and the briars inert. The only motion within the charmed circle was the rise and fall of his arm and the shifting of the cut stems as he pushed them aside. The sounds of the wind and the thrashing briars were clear but faint, as if they came from outside the walls of a sturdy house. The thud of his ax, the rustle of the briars as he passed, and the crunch of his boots against the mountainside were, in contrast, clear and precise, like the sound of Una's singing in a quiet room. Dreamlike, Arven glided onward, moving surely despite the gloom. His ax, too, never missed a stroke, though as the keep drew nearer, the night thickened until the faint light of the stars no longer penetrated its blackness.

Arven had no idea how long he spent carving his path through the snarl of briars. His arms grew tired, but his strokes never lost their rhythm and his steps never faltered. Even when he came to the ditch that surrounded the castle, three man-heights deep and nearly as wide, and so steep-sided that a mountain goat might have had difficulty with the climb, his progress slowed only a little. The briars grew more sparsely in the thin soil that veiled the rocky sides of the ditch, and now and again Arven left a stem in place, to catch at his sleeves and the back of his coat and help keep him from slipping.

He reached the bottom of the ditch at last and paused to catch his breath. He could feel the keep looming above him and hear the rushing wind and the thrashing of the briars, though he could see none of them. He wondered what would happen if he lost his direction, and was suddenly glad of the ditch. It was a landmark that could not be mistaken, even in such blackness; if he climbed the wrong side, his mistake would be obvious as soon as he got to the top, and he would only have to retrace his steps.

"Go on," the prince's voice whispered in his ear.

Arven jumped, having all but forgotten the other's presence. There was exhaustion in that voice, a deeper exhaustion by far than the world-weary undertone it had had when Arven first heard it, and in his concern he almost turned to offer the prince his arm. Just in time, he remembered the prince's warning.

"Put your hand through my belt," Arven said, forgetting his own fatigue. "We've a climb ahead, and you'll keep up better if I tow you a way."

The prince did not answer. Arven waited, but he felt no tug at his belt. "Stubborn young fool," he muttered. Holding back the briars must be more tiring than the prince had expected. Arven tried not to think of what would happen if the prince's magic failed before they got to the keep. Well, if the prince was too proud to admit he needed help, Arven had better finish his part of the business as quickly as he could. He raised his ax and started forward once more.

Climbing out of the ditch took even longer than climbing into it had done. Arven's weariness had taken firm hold on him during the brief rest, and his arms were nearly too tired to swing his ax. His back ached and his legs felt as if his boots were weighted with lead. He let himself sink into a kind of daze, repeating the same movements over and over without thinking.

The jolt of his ax striking unyielding stone instead of wood brought Arven out of his trance. He cursed himself for a fool; that stroke had blunted the ax for certain. He probed for a moment with the flat of the blade and realized abruptly that this was no random protruding rock. He had arrived at the outer wall of the keep.

Arven felt along the wall a few feet in both directions, but found no sign of a gate or door. The briars grew only to within two feet of the wall, leaving a narrow path along the top of the ditch. Without looking back, he called an explanation to the prince, then turned left and started sunwise around the keep, one hand on the wall.

He had not gone far when the wall bulged outward. He followed the curve, and as he came around the far side he felt the ground smooth out beneath his feet. The wind that whipped the briars ceased as though a door had been shut on it, and silence fell with shocking suddenness. A moment later, the prince said, "This is the gate. We can rest here for a few minutes, if you like."

Arven looked over his shoulder. The night seemed less dense now; he could just make out the prince's silhouette, charcoal gray against midnight blackness. He stood squarely in the center of an arched opening through which Arven had passed without noticing. Though the prince's voice was more tired than ever, Arven could see no trace of weariness in his stance.

"What else must we face?" Arven asked, leaning against the crumbling wall.

"Only finding the count's daughter and waking her," the prince said. "Whatever is left in the keep is not dangerous, though it may be unpleasant."

"Then there's no point in lingering," Arven said.

"Light the lantern, and we'll start looking for the girl."

There was a long pause. "I didn't bring the lantern."

"Young idiot," Arven said without heat. He should have thought to mention it; he was old enough to know better than to rely on an untutored and romantically inclined youth to think of practical matters. He smiled. He was old enough to know better than to try and penetrate the briars around the keep, too, but here he was. "I suppose we could just wait for dawn."

"No!" The prince took a quick step, as if he would shove Arven on by main force. "I can't—I mean, I don't—"

Knowing that the prince could not see him, Arven let his smile grow broader. "Well enough," he said, trying to keep the smile from showing in his voice. "I can understand why you'd be eager to have this finished. But while we look for your girl, keep an eye out for a torch or a lamp or something. I've no mind to come this far just to break a leg on the stairs for lack of light."

"As you wish," the prince said. "Are you rested?"

Arven laughed. "As much as I'm likely to be." He pushed himself away from the wall and started off. He kept one hand on the stone as he walked, feeling the texture change as he passed under the supporting arches. Despite his care, he stumbled and nearly fell a moment later. When he felt for the obstruction that had tripped him, he found a well-rotted stump of wood leaning against a heavy iron bar—all that was left of the first door. With a shrug, he rose and entered the outer bailey.

As he did, something brushed his face. He jerked and swiped at it one-handed and found himself holding a handful of leaves.

"Ivy," said the prince from behind him, and Arven jumped again. "It's not the climbing sort; it grows in cracks between the stones above and hangs down."

"I know the plant," Arven said shortly. He threw the leaves away and looked up. A few yards ahead, the curved sides of the inner gatehouse rose dizzily above him and flattened briefly into the inner wall before bulging out into the round corner towers. This close, the gatehouse blotted out the shapes of the mountains. Its dark surface was broken only by the darker slots of the arrow loops and a few irregular clumps of ivy, swaying gently.

Arven blinked and realized that the darkness was fading. He could see the stars behind the towers, and there was a faint, pale haze in the sky that hinted at the coming of dawn in an hour or two. Somewhere a bird chirped sleepily.

"We must hurry," the prince said. "Come." He started for the twin towers of the inner gatehouse, and Arven followed. His part in this adventure might be over, but he had earned the right to see the end of it.

"There is work for your ax here," the prince called from the tunnel that led between the towers to the inner part of the keep.

Arven snorted at himself and quickened his step. When he reached the prince's side, the difficulty was clear. The first portcullis was down, but closer examination showed that the iron bands had rusted and sprung apart and the wooden grate was all askew and rotten besides. A few careful ax strokes cleared the way with ease. The second portcullis, at the far end of the tunnel-like entrance, had fallen and jammed partway. Arven ducked under the spikes and stepped out into the inner bailey.

Another bird chirped from somewhere on the wall above his head, and another. Arven had never understood why birds insisted on chattering at each other from the moment the night sky began to lighten. Surely dawn was early enough! He turned to point out the perversity of birds to the prince and did not see him.

"Your Highness?"

"Here." The prince waved from the door of the gatehouse. "There are candles."

"Good." The door was half ajar. Arven shoved it wide and peered in, then recoiled. Two skeletons lay sprawled across the table in the center of the room, white bones protruding from rotting shreds of livery.

Arven looked reproachfully at the prince. "You might have warned me."

"I didn't think." The prince sounded as much worried as apologetic. "They are only dead, after all."

"Next time, get the candles yourself, then," Arven snapped. He went in and retrieved two fat, stubby candles and a rusty iron holder, fixed one of the candles in place, and lit it with some difficulty.

The prince was waiting for him in the bailey. "The count's daughter will be somewhere in the great hall, I think," he said, pointing. "I . . . expect there will be more such as those."

"Dead men, you mean."

The prince nodded. "The spell—the curse— should have protected the whole of the keep, but it has gone on too long. I doubt there is anyone living, except the girl."

"Let's find her, then, and leave this place to the ghosts."

The prince winced, then nodded again. "As you say. Lead on."

"I?"

"You have the light."

Arven shot a glare at the prince, though he knew the effect would be lost in the darkness. There was nothing he could say to such a reasonable request, however, so he did as the prince had suggested.

The door to the great hall was made of solid oak

planks, a little weathered but still more than service-able. It took most of Arven's remaining strength to wrestle it open. He threw another glare in the prince's direction; the man couldn't be any more tired than Arven, no matter how wearing magic was. The prince did not seem to notice.

Inside, the main room was eerily still. On the far side, the window glass had shattered, letting in star-light and the small noises of wind and birds. Closer by, long tables filled the center of the room and the candlelight struck glints from gold and silver plate. Around the tables, and sometimes over them, lay a collection of black, shapeless figures. A faint, sweetish odor of decay hung in the air, and Arven grimaced. He skirted the edge of the room, avoiding the tables and taking care to shield the candle so that he would not see the details of the anonymous forms.

"There will be stairs in the corner," the prince said.

Arven found them: a narrow stone spiral built into the wall of the keep itself. He started up, his shoulders brushing the wall on one side and the central pillar on the other. The steps were as steep as the rocks of the upper mountain, and the climb was awkward. More than once, Arven wished he could lean forward a few inches more and climb on all fours, as if he were going up a ladder or scaling a cliff. He wondered whether castle folk ever became accustomed to the tight, cir-cular ascent. Did they think no more of it than Arven did of shinning up a tree to cut away an inconvenient branch that might affect its fall? The prince, at least, did not seem bothered.

Around and around they went, passing one door after another, until Arven lost track of how far they had come. At each door, Arven stopped to ask, "This one?" Each time, the prince shook his head and they went on. Finally, they reached the top of the stairs. This time, Arven pushed the door open without asking; there was, after all, no other place to go.

He found himself in a narrow hall. "The far end," the prince said, and Arven went on. He found a door and pushed it open, and stopped, staring.

The chamber was small and cluttered. Broken boards leaned against one wall, some carved, others plain. A stool with a broken leg was propped on a circular washtub; next to it was a chair with only one arm. A stack of table trestles filled one corner, and a pile of rolled-up rugs and tapestries took up another. Old rope hung in dusty loops from a peg beside the window, and the window ledge was full of dented pewter and cracked pottery.

The center of the room had been cleared in haste by someone unconcerned with niceties of order. In the middle of the open space stood a broken spinning wheel. One leg was missing and two of the spokes were broken; the treadle dangled on a bent wire and the driving cord was gone. Only the spindle shone bright and sharp and new. Beside the spinning wheel, a girl lay in a crumpled heap, one hand stretched out as if to catch herself and a tumbled mass of black hair hiding her face.

Arven set the candle holder on top of the stack of table trestles and bent over the girl. Gently, he slid an arm under her. His work-roughened fingers caught on the heavy, old-fashioned brocade of her dress as he lifted her and turned her shoulders so that he could see her face.

She was beautiful. He had expected that; nobleman's daughters were nearly always beautiful, protected as they were from the ravages of sun and illness and general hardship. But he had not expected to find such determination in the pointed pixie chin, or such character in the fine bones of her face. Arven tore his eyes away and turned to the prince.

The prince stood in the doorway, watching the girl with such love and longing that Arven almost averted his eyes to keep from intruding on what should be private. "Well?" Arven said gruffly.

"Kiss her," said the prince, and looked away.

Arven stared, astonished. "Do it yourself. That's why you came, surely."

"I can't." The prince's voice was hardly more than a whisper.

"Can't? What do you—" Arven broke off as the prince raised his hand and stretched it toward the candle. Suddenly the pieces came together and Arven knew, even before he saw the candle gleaming through the translucent flesh, even before he watched the prince's hand grasp the holder and pass through it without touching. *No wonder he would not carry the lantern,* Arven thought, *no wonder he could only work the spell at night,* and marveled that he could be so calm.

"Please, it's almost dawn," the prince said. He gestured toward the window. The sky beyond was visibly paler. "Kiss her and break the curse, so that I can see the end of this before I must go." His eyes were on the girl's face again, and this time Arven did look away.

"Please," the prince repeated after a moment.

Arven nodded without looking up. Awkwardly, he bent and kissed the girl full on the lips.

For a long moment, nothing seemed to happen. Then there was a grinding sound from somewhere below, and a loud crash, and the girl heaved a sigh. Her eyelids flickered, then opened. As she looked at Arven, an expression of puzzlement crossed her face. She sat up, and glanced around, and saw the prince. Their eyes locked, and she stiffened, and Arven knew that, somehow, she understood.

"Thank you," the girl said.

"Thank him," said the prince. "He broke the curse. I did nothing."

Arven made a gesture of protest that neither of them saw.

"You came back," the girl told the prince with

calm certainty. "That is a great deal more than nothing."

The prince went still. "How did you know?"

"I know." She rose and brushed her skirts, then gave the prince a deep and graceful curtsy. The prince stretched out a protesting hand, and the girl smiled like sun on morning dew. "And I thank you for it."

"You should blame me. If I had done it right the first time, there would have been no need for these makeshifts."

"True." The girl's smile vanished and she looked at him gravely. "I think perhaps you owe me something after all, for that."

The prince gave her a bitter smile. "What is it you want of me, lady?"

"Wait for me."

The prince stared, uncomprehending, but Arven understood at once. It was what he had asked of Una, at the last. *Wait for me, if you can.*

"It won't be long," the girl continued. "I can feel it."

"You have a lifetime ahead of you!" the prince said.

"A lifetime can be two days long; it needs only a birth at the beginning and a death at the end." The girl smiled again, without bitterness. "By any usual reckoning, I have had more than my share of lifetimes."

"The spell . . ."

"Was unraveling. If you had not come, I should have slept another hundred years, or two, dying slowly with no company but dreams. I have learned a great deal from my dreams, but I prefer waking, if only for a week or a month."

"I see." The prince reached out as if to stroke her hair, but stopped his hand just short of its unattainable goal. Arven could see the curve of the girl's shoulder clearly through the prince's palm. He glanced at the window. The sky was lightening rapidly.

"Then, will you wait?" the girl asked again.

"I will try," said the prince. He was almost completely transparent by this time, and his voice was as faint as the distant breeze that rustled the trees outside the keep.

"Try hard," the girl said seriously.

Arven had to squint to see the prince nod, and then the sky was bright with dawn and the prince had vanished. The girl turned away, but not before Arven caught the glitter of tears in her eyes. He rose and picked up the candle, unsure of how to proceed.

"I have not thanked you, woodcutter," the girl said at last, turning. "Forgive me, and do believe I am grateful."

"It's no matter," Arven said. "I understand."

She smiled at him. "Then let us go down. It has been a long time since I have seen the dawn from the castle wall."

CRUEL SISTERS

THE HARPER WOULD HAVE YOU believe that it was all for the love of sweet William that my sisters came to hate each other so, but that is not true. They were bitter rivals from the time we were very small. His song misleads about other things, too; it does not mention me, for instance. "Two sisters in a bower," it says, not three, though the harp spoke of me and the harper himself stood beside my chair that day when he and his harp turned our clean grief to bitter poison. As for what the song says of William—well, the harper did not write that part himself, so he is not wholly to blame. I could forgive him for that, but not for what he said of my sisters.

Anne was the eldest of us three. Everyone who saw her said she was born to be a queen, with her long black hair and dark, flashing eyes, and her intelligence and force of will. When first they met her, people came away thinking that she was tall; it was always a shock to them to see her again in company and find that she was barely average woman-size. Eleanor was the tall one; after she passed Anne in height, she made me mark the lintel of our chamber every week for two years, until she finally tired of taunting Anne. In other ways, too, Eleanor was Anne's opposite: her hair was golden, and her eyes a clear, cornflower blue. If Anne was born to be a queen, Eleanor was meant to be a rich duke's pampered wife, carefree and merry.

And I? I am Margaret, plain Meg, in all things the middle daughter. My hair is thick, but it is an ordinary brown. My face is pleasant enough, I think, but that is a far cry from my sisters' beauty. My father calls me the quiet one, when he thinks of me; my mother says I am too much on the sidelines, watching and thinking and saying little. By the common wisdom, it should have been I who was jealous of my sisters, but I loved them both, and even when we were children it hurt me to watch the spiteful tricks they played on each other.

They loved me, too, in their own ways. Sometimes, rarely, one would even give up tormenting the other if I asked it, but such occasions grew less frequent as we grew older. The last time I tried to intervene was when Anne was fourteen and Eleanor twelve.

Eleanor had spilled ink on her best dress and laid the blame on Anne. Anne said nothing when our tutor punished her for it, but her lips were stiff and white about the edges. I did not know, then, that Eleanor had lied about the ink, but I knew that something was very wrong.

That afternoon, I missed them both, a circumstance so unusual that I went looking for them at once. I found them outside the curtain wall, in the far garden beside the river, where the briars are left to ramble as they will. Anne had Eleanor's favorite gown—not her best one, which had the ink spilled on it, but the blue silk the color of her eyes, with the white roses embroidered about the neck—and was waving it beside the thorns while Eleanor wept and snatched at it, trying to keep it from harm. Neither of them saw me as I came near.

"You lied to Master Crombie," Anne said, waving the dress. "Admit it."

"You know whether I did or not," Eleanor said. "Give me my gown!"

"Lies are beneath the dignity of our house," Anne said coldly. "One who bears our name ought not to lie."

"Eleanor!" I said, and they both turned to look at me. "Is it true?"

"Is what true?" she said, but her eyes slid away from mine, and I knew that Anne was right, that Eleanor had indeed made up the tale she told our tutor.

"She told Master Crombie that I had ruined her gown," Anne said in a grim tone. "It was not true when she said it, but I will make it true now." And she made to throw the fragile blue silk among the thorns.

"No!" I said, and she paused and looked at me.

"You take her side?"

I shook my head. "No. What she did was wrong. But what you would do will not make it right."

"I will tell Master Crombie the truth," Eleanor said suddenly, her eyes fixed on Anne's hands.

Anne turned, looked startled, and her grip loosened. Eleanor darted forward and seized the gown, then whirled away, laughing. "Silly, foolish, to be so tricked!"

Anne's lips went white, and she lunged forward. I was just too late to stop her. With all her might, she shoved Eleanor into the briars. Eleanor screamed in fright and pain as the thorns scratched her and tore her skirts.

"Now the things you told Master Crombie are true, after all," Anne said to her. "I have made them so."

"Anne!" I said. "How could you? Eleanor, be still! You will only hurt yourself if you thrash about."

"Let her hurt as much as I did when Master Crombie whipped me for her lies," Anne said.

"She might have been hurt far worse," I said as I went to help Eleanor out of the briars. "Men have been blinded in those thorns." I kept my voice as calm as I could, though I was deeply shocked by both their actions. I think they saw it, but neither would apologize, or admit to being in the wrong, and from that day, whatever power I might once have had to stop them hurting one another, I had no longer.

I do not know what tale Eleanor made to account for her scratches and the rips in two of her gowns, but I know it was not the truth, for neither she nor Anne was ever disciplined for it. Indeed, if I had not been there myself, I would not have known why Eleanor no longer wore her favorite blue gown. Perhaps I would not have noticed the increased tension between my sisters, either. No one else seemed aware of it, though to me the atmosphere in the schoolroom seemed to grow daily more fraught with anger and resentment.

So I was happy when Anne was finally old enough to put up her hair and move on to grown-up things, for it meant that the fights between her and Eleanor all but ceased. I thought their enmity must end with growing up, and for a few years it seemed to do so. I made my own transition to the world of feasts and dancing smoothly. I watched Anne with her suitors, but, as befits a younger sister, I sought none of my own until she should have made her choice.

And then William came to court. "Sweet William," some of the verses say, and another song styles him "bonny William, brave and true." Well, he was bonny enough, with his gray eyes and hair like the silk on corn, and he had a tongue like honey, but from the first I did not like him. I had spent my early years watching my lovely sisters wound each other with comments no one else could see were barbed; perhaps it gave me a distrust of beauty and sweet words. But if that were so, Anne should have been armored even better than I, and she loved him from the moment he bent to kiss her hand before leading her out for their first dance.

"Isn't he handsome?" she said to me that night as we made ready for bed. "And kind. And a little shy, I think."

"He didn't seem shy to me when he was flirting with the serving maid," I said.

"Meg! He did no such thing." Anne sounded really distressed. "You're making it up."

"I know what I saw."

"He may have talked with her, but it was just to put her at ease," Anne said. "I told you he was kind. You must have misinterpreted it."

"I suppose I might have," I said, though I was sure I had not. Anne's expression lightened at once, and she went on singing William's praises until the maids came to put out the rushlights. She did not seem to notice my lack of response, or if she did, she put it down to tact or sympathy. But I do not think she noticed. She was too full of William.

"He is not the only man who courted you this evening," I said at last. "Robert brought you roses, and Malcolm—"

"Feh to Robert and Malcolm and all the rest," Anne said. "William is my choice, and I'll have him or no one."

"You can't mean that, Anne!" I said, appalled. "It is too sudden."

"Oh, I'll not be so hasty before the court," she said. "Did you think I meant to claim him tomorrow? We'll have a decorous courtship, and when he speaks to Father at last, no one will be amazed or put out. But I wanted you to know."

"You've not planned it out between you already?" I said. "After only one meeting?"

Anne laughed. "You are a goose. Go to sleep, and dream which of the men you will choose to look kindly on when I am settled. Robert, perhaps, since his roses made such an impression on you."

I threw a pillow at her. It was not until later, when she was asleep, that I realized she had not answered my question.

Anne was as good as her word. Over the next six weeks, she let her partiality for William begin to show, slowly but certainly, so that soon there was no doubt in anyone's mind that William was to be my father's first son-in-law. Before the court, she was discreet; when we were alone and private at night, she filled my ears with William's excellencies. They planned for William to make a formal request for her hand before the assembled May Day Court, in another month. And then Eleanor's birthday arrived, and she put up her hair for her coming-of-age feast.

I should have guessed what would happen. Gossip travels on the air in a king's hall; even in the schoolroom, Eleanor must have heard of Anne and William and their coming handfasting. Coming, but not yet concluded. Hating Anne as she did, as she had for so long, it was inevitable that she would try to spoil her happiness.

In all fairness, she did not have to try very hard. William took one look at Eleanor and fell as hard and far as Anne had fallen for him. And he was not in the least discreet about the change in the object of his affections. Indeed, it must have been plain even to Anne that he had never truly cared for her, for he had never treated her with half the tenderness he used toward Eleanor.

When I saw how it would be, I went to Eleanor and begged her to relent, for all our sakes. She smiled at me and shook her head. "It is too late for that. William loves me, not Anne."

"Yes, but the pair of you need not flaunt it before her," I said. I was angry, and sore on Anne's behalf, and I spoke more sharply than I had intended.

Eleanor looked startled. "Is that what you think? That we have been brandishing our affection apurpose?"

Then I saw that she had not; it was only her usual heedlessness. I said, "It is what Anne thinks."

"Oh, Anne. She has grieved me enough in my life; this time it is her turn."

"Do not say that," I said, distressed. "Love should not serve spite, and she is your sister, as much as I am." *And you have given her grief for grief, all your lives,* I could have added, but did not.

"Dear Meg," Eleanor said. "Always the peace-maker. Well, I suppose I can do that much for you. But I cannot give him up now, even if I would. He will not have it so."

"I know," I said. "I wish he had never come here."

So, on the first of May, before the assembled court, William asked my father for Eleanor's hand, not Anne's. It was scandalous, of course—the youngest daughter to be married before either of her sisters!—but there was already so much scandal about the match that it hardly mattered. Anne was pale as milk, but she kept her head high. Only I knew how she wept in the garden afterward, and only I seemed to notice the white stiffness around her lips, which I had not seen since that day when she pushed Eleanor into the briars.

It was that memory that sent me to Eleanor once again, to beg her to make peace with Anne. Yet I was surprised when she agreed; I had not expected her to hear my plea. I did not expect Anne to listen, either, but she did. I wonder, now, if things would have happened as they did, had I not interfered. Perhaps Eleanor wanted only to gloat over her latest and most final victory, and not to mend matters as she said she would; perhaps Anne wanted to vent her anger and pain, and not to ease her heart. There is no way to know. I tell myself that if those things were true, what I did can have made no real difference. But I do not really believe it.

All the world knows what happened next: how Anne and Eleanor went walking by the river that ran dark and swollen with snowmelt, and how only Anne returned, her dress torn, her hands scratched, and her hair in wild disarray. She told us Eleanor had slipped and fallen into the torrent, and she had struggled through the briars along the bank, trying without success to pull her out.

My father sent his men off to search at once, of course. William was first among them, his eyes a little wild, and Anne looked away as he rode out. Then she collapsed, all in a heap. I was almost glad. Tending Anne gave me something to do while we waited for the men to return.

They returned without Eleanor. I heard one of them say that with the river swollen as it was, she had doubtless been swept out to sea. Anne heard, too, and we wept together. Father sent more men for boats, though he must have known by then that it was hopeless. "At least we can bring her back to the churchyard," he said, and his voice cracked when he spoke.

We were not allowed even so much as that. My father's men found nothing, though the fisherfolk, too, joined in the search. Three days later, there was a terrible storm, with wind and hail and lightning and the sea in a wild rage. Afterward, everyone could see that little likelihood remained of finding Eleanor's body. The priest said a memorial mass, and my father paid him for a year of daily prayers. Things began to slip back into the routine of ordinary days, save that when we glanced out at the kitchen garden, or in at the sewing rooms, or down the long high table, we did not see Eleanor's bright hair, nor thought we ever would again.

Anne took it hardest of us all. She picked at her food but ate little, and she slept hardly at all. After that first day, she never spoke of Eleanor but once. "She was so frightened," Anne told me, "and I could not pull her out. I could not."

I did not know how to comfort her. Indeed, I was surprised that she should need comforting. The rest of the court might marvel at her devotion to her youngest sister, but I knew how little love had been lost between them. I thought it was the horror of watching Eleanor drown that shadowed Anne's eyes, and perhaps it was. Or perhaps she was lost without Eleanor to rail against. Perhaps.

A month went by, and the grief of Eleanor's passing was no longer a sharp knife in the heart, but a dull, heavy burden that ached the muscles and tired the spirit. William stayed at court, and now and then I saw him watching Anne covertly. He had loved Eleanor, I was sure, but Eleanor was gone and he still wished to marry one of my father's daughters. It was too soon for him to transfer his affections back. Nonetheless, he could watch and judge his chances.

I did not think they were good. Anne was not one to take such a slight as he had put on her and then return to him smiling when he crooked his finger. William did not understand that. Once, he tried to speak with her, and she walked away without answering. Later in the evening, I heard him telling Robert that it touched his heart to see how Anne grieved for his Eleanor. He knew that I was near, and he spoke louder than he needed; I think he meant for me to carry tales to Anne. But that I could not do, even if I would have. Anne spoke no more of William than she did of Eleanor. It was as if they had both died, together, in that swollen river.

And then, suddenly, Midsummer was upon us. As was the custom, my father planned a feast, though none of us rejoiced in the prospect. It was to be the first great feast since Eleanor's death, and everywhere we turned we were reminded anew that she was no longer there.

To turn our minds from the empty place at the high table, my father sent out word that any harpers who wished to join us would be welcomed and would have a chance to play before the king and queen and their daughters. Harpers are always guested and gifted, of course, for harpers are known to hold some of the old magic and it is ill luck to do otherwise, but in the normal course of things only the best perform in the great hall. My mother complained of it, when she heard. She said we would spend an evening listening to every bad and boring player who earned a bit of bread on the highways and in the taverns, but by then it was too late to take back the offer.

For the most part, she was right. The harpers nearly outnumbered the guests at our Midsummer feast, and though Father set a limit of two songs apiece, each seemed to have chosen the two longest and most boring pieces he knew. It was nearing midnight when the last man rose to take his seat and play for us.

He was a tall man, blond and full of bony angles. He did not move with the practiced grace of the other musicians, and he carried his harp case as if it were an infant.

"My lord king, I bring you a wonder," he said,

and even in those simple words, his voice was gold and silk.

My father nodded. "Sit and play for us, harper."

"I shall not play, my lord, but you shall hear a song the like of which no man has heard before."

"If you do not play, why do you carry a harp?" my father asked.

"It is the harp that plays," the minstrel said. His voice deepened and seemed to call shadows from all the corners of the room. "Listen, O king! For this is no ordinary harp. I made it of the bones of a drowned maiden I found upon the seashore and strung it with her hair, and as I worked I sang the ancient songs of magic, that the harp might sing in its turn. And now, indeed, it does. Hear the tale, and marvel!"

With that, he opened the harp case with a flourish and set his instrument on the stone floor before him. He did not seem to notice the horror that dawned upon the faces of our guests at his bald claim, or the way my father's face had gone white when he mentioned the drowned girl, or how my mother swayed in her seat when he told what gruesome use he made of the body. His attention was all on the harp.

A moment later, so was ours, for as soon as the minstrel stepped back, the harp began to play itself. One after another, the strings sang in notes of piercing strangeness, sweeter and more biting than the music of any ordinary harp. They filled the hall and echoed in the flickering shadows. The notes ran up and down the scale, then began to play a simple song, a tune that all of us had heard a hundred times and more. But the words that sang among the notes were no song any of us had heard before, and the voice that sang them . . . the voice was Eleanor's.

> *"Mother and father, queen and king,*
> *Farewell to you, farewell I sing.*
> *Farewell to William, sweet and true,*
> *Farewell, dear sister Meg, to you.*
> *But woe to my fair sister Anne*
> *Who killed me for to take my man."*

The harp played its scale once more and then began to repeat the verse. We sat frozen, all of us—all of us but Anne. She rose, her lips white and stiff, and walked to the harp. As it reached the final lines, the lines that named her Eleanor's murderer, Anne picked up the harp and smashed it against the hearthstone with all her might.

The bone splintered, stopping the music in a jangling discord. The jarring noises hung in the air long after Anne turned to face the assembled guests once more. She stood there, her chin high, every inch a king's daughter, while the last lingering sounds died into silence and the silence stretched into dismay and horror.

It was the minstrel who broke the silence. "You

have killed your sister a second time," he said to Anne in his beautiful, silken voice.

Anne looked at him coldly. "Then that much of what she sang is true, now."

My mother slid to the floor in a faint. My father stood, though he had to brace himself against the table to keep his feet without trembling. "Take her away," he said in a hoarse voice.

"No!" I said before I thought.

He turned to look at me. "Margaret, it must be," he said, and his tone was gentle, though I could see the effort it took for him to speak so. "You heard the harp. See to your mother." He turned back to the hall and repeated, "Take her away."

The guards moved forward jerkily, like ill-managed puppets. I looked away, for I could not bear to watch. They took Anne quickly from the hall, and as the door closed behind them, the guests unfroze and began to murmur in low, stricken tones. I could not bear that, either. My mother's ladies were all around her, leaving nothing for me to do. I rose to leave.

The minstrel stood beside the door, holding his empty harp case. He looked at me with sympathy. I think that under other circumstances, I might have liked him. "It is hard for you to compass," he said softly. "I am sorry for your hurt."

I am not so good as Anne at giving people a look or a glare that freezes them to the bone, but I did the best I could. "You desecrated my sister's body, and for what? To cut up our peace and raise doubts where there were none."

"To find out the truth," the minstrel said, but he sounded a little shaken.

"The truth? What truth? My sister Eleanor was a liar all her life, and all her life cast the blame for her own errors on Anne. Why should death have changed that?"

"The dead are beyond such pettiness."

"Are they?" I said. "For most of what the harp sang, I do not know, but this much you can hear from anyone at court: 'William, sweet and true' was true to neither Anne nor Eleanor. And if the harp lied about that, why not about the other matters?"

I left while he was still casting about for an answer. I was tired and sore at heart and much confused. I did not know what to believe. Eleanor was a liar, and I know better than anyone the lengths to which she would go to spite Anne. But Anne had a temper, and when it was roused . . . well, I could not help remembering the briars. She might have pushed Eleanor into the river the same way and regretted it after. She might have. But did she?

We buried the shattered remains of the harp, which were all we had of my sister's bones. The ceremony brought no one any peace or comfort. The memories of magic and possible murder clung too close, and the tiny coffin made everyone think of the minstrel plucking and coiling Eleanor's golden hair for harp strings, and shaping her finger bones into tuning pegs, and cutting apart her breastbone for the harp itself. It would have been better if someone had thought to use a coffin of ordinary size. At least then we could have pretended to forget what had been done to her.

They could not try Anne for murder on the strength of a harp song, and that was all the proof they had. Still, after such an accusation, made in such a way, something had to be done. In the end, my father sent her to a convent to do penance among the sisters. She died of a chill less than six months later. She never denied what the harp had said, any more than she had ever denied Eleanor's lies in public. But the sisters say that she never confessed her guilt, either.

And I? I am the only daughter now, and it is a hard position to fill alone. William, "bonny William, brave and true," gave the lie to the harp's description once more by making sheep's eyes at me almost before the convent doors had closed behind Anne. I sent him away, and I was firm enough about it that he has not returned, for which I am grateful. But there will be others like him soon enough.

Even those who see me, Margaret, and not merely the king's last daughter, do not understand. They say I grieve too long for my sisters, that I should put their tragedy behind me. I grieve for Eleanor and Anne, yes, but it is my own guilt that takes me to the chapel every morning. If I had spoken sooner, if I had made our nurses and our tutors and our parents see the depth of the rivalry between Anne and Eleanor, perhaps one of them could have put a stop to it before it ended in this horror. At the least, perhaps they would have listened when I tried to make them see that the harp was not to be believed without question.

It is too late to change what happened between my sisters, but I still hear more than others seem to, and I have begun to speak of what I hear. It is hard to break the habit of so many years, but I think that I am getting better at it. At least, my efforts now have met with more success than did my attempts to soothe my sisters. Lord Owen and Lord Douglas set their argument aside after I spoke with them last month. My father says I stopped a potential feud, and speaks of having me attend the next working court, to advise him about the petitioners. So much attention makes me uncomfortable, but I suppose I shall become accustomed in time. It is the price I must pay for saying what I know. And if I have learned anything from this, I have learned that it is not enough to see. One must speak out as well.

Even today, I do not know what happened that day beside the river. But I am the only one with doubts, it seems. The dramatic accusation persuaded nearly everyone, and those who were not satisfied by the harp's song were convinced when Anne smashed the harp to bits. She did it to silence her accuser, they say. But I remember her words to the minstrel: "Then that much of what she sang is true, now." And I remember her voice when she was fourteen, saying of Eleanor, "It was not true when she said it, but I will make it true now."

I tried to tell my father all my doubts before he sent Anne away, as I tried to tell the minstrel that night in the great hall. Father would not listen then; like everyone else, he believed the harp. The minstrel's hearing was better, I think. For though the song he wrote afterward tells only the story that everyone believes, and nothing of the doubts I shared with him, he has at least made no more magic harps from the desecrated bodies of the dead.

UTENSILE STRENGTH

QUEEN CIMORENE OF THE Enchanted Forest stepped
back and cocked her head to one side, setting her black
braids swinging. "A little to the left, dear," she said.

Obligingly, her husband moved the large, gold-
framed painting.

"A little more. Yes, that's perfect. Now, if you'll
just hold it a minute longer—"

Behind her, there was a discreet cough. "Your
Majesty."

The King and Queen turned their heads simulta-
neously to find a plump, gray-haired elf in green velvet
and lace ruffles standing in the doorway. "Yes?" they
both said at the same time.

The elf bowed immediately. "Ah, Your Majesties, I should say."

"Yes, Willin, what *is* it?" said the King. "And can't it wait another ten minutes?"

"I'm sure I didn't mean to disturb Your Majesties," Willin said.

"Put the picture down, Mendanbar," Cimorene said with a sigh. "There's no point in arguing with Willin. Or hurrying him. He's as stubborn as I am."

"Nobody's as stubborn as you are, dear heart, and I'm not putting this down just when we've finally gotten it in the right place. Daystar! Here, Daystar, we want you."

With a soft popping noise and a brief eddy of air, Prince Daystar appeared in the center of the room. He had Cimorene's black hair and Mendanbar's long, lanky build, and though he was still shorter than his parents, he had the slightly awkward look of someone who hadn't finished growing. "Yes, Father? What is it?"

"Just stick this picture to the wall, will you? My hands are full, or I'd do it myself."

The Prince nodded and gestured with one hand. A moment later, Mendanbar let go of the painting and flexed his fingers with a relieved sigh. The painting stayed where it was, just as if it had been hung on a nail.

"Thank you," Mendanbar said to Daystar. "Now, Willin, what was it you wanted?"

"There is a . . . a young man at the door, Your Majesty, insisting on seeing you," the elf said in evident disapproval.

"At the door?" Cimorene said. "Willin, I'm ashamed of you. It's pouring rain outside. Go and let him in immediately."

"I was using the phrase as a figure of speech," Willin said stiffly. "The young man is currently standing in the hallway, dripping on the handmade silk rug that the Emperor of the Indies presented to His Majesty's grandmother. He is insisting on speaking with His Majesty."

"It's a very ugly rug," Mendanbar said. "That's why we put it in the entry hall."

"Did he say what he wanted?" Daystar asked.

"Something about a frying pan," the elf said in a gloomy tone.

"He's probably come to apply for a job in the kitchen," Cimorene said. "We still need a third assistant cook and two scullery maids, and I told the head cook I want to interview them myself. I refuse to let him hire a princess in disguise who's hoping to sneak into the next ball wearing a dress as shining as the stars so that Daystar will fall in love with her. Princesses are very persuasive, but most of them aren't much use in the kitchen."

Daystar blinked. "But Mother, we hardly ever have balls. And I really don't think I'd fall in love with someone just because she was wearing a fancy dress."

"Try and convince a princess of that."

"You'd better bring the gentleman in," Mendanbar said to Willin.

The elf hesitated. "Now, Your Majesty? Here?"

"Yes, of course," Mendanbar said, puzzled.

"It's all right, Willin," Cimorene said. "He'll put on his crown before you get back."

"Very well, Your Majesties. Your Highness." Willin bowed to everyone in turn and left.

Mendanbar looked after him with a thoughtful expression. "Poor Willin. I don't think he's ever going to get used to me."

"He likes formality, and you have to admit that you're dressed a little more casually than is common among royalty." Cimorene nodded at his stained brown smock.

"I'm not going to dress in velvet robes with ermine trim when I'm spending the day hanging pictures and cleaning out the attic in the South Tower, no matter how much Willin would like it," Mendanbar said firmly.

"I think the real problem is that he doesn't think a king should be hanging pictures and cleaning out attics," Daystar said.

"He's wrong," Cimorene said flatly. "But you *did* say you'd put your crown on to receive visitors, dear."

"No, you said that." Nonetheless, Mendanbar made a quick, complex gesture like pulling on invisible cords. An instant later, two crowns appeared in the air in front of him. He caught them and handed one to his wife. "Fair is fair. If I have to wear one, you have to wear one, too."

Cimorene smiled and took it. They settled the crowns on their heads just as Willin came through the doorway once more. With him was a solidly built young man with sandy brown hair, carrying a large cast-iron frying pan.

"Your Majesties, Your Highness, Tamriff of High Holes wishes an audience."

"Thank you, Willin," said the King. "What did you want to see us about, Tamriff?"

"This," Tamriff replied, carefully raising the frying pan. When he held it up, they could all see that he wore a large brown oven mitt on the hand holding the pan.

"That is not a suitable subject for discussion with the King of the Enchanted Forest," Willin said huffily.

"Yes, it is," Daystar said. "It's a magic frying pan."

Tamriff looked at him with respect. "How did you know that?"

"It's sort of a knack."

"What does it do?" Cimorene said. "Make gourmet meals, or just instant eggs-and-bacon for however many people you need to feed?"

Tamriff sighed. "No. That's the problem. It's a weapon."

"A weapon? It's a *frying pan*."

"My father is an enchanter," Tamriff explained. "A couple of years ago, he decided that he was going to create the ultimate weapon, something powerful and wondrous that heroes would fight over for centuries. The Sword of Doom, he wanted to call it. Only Mother came in with the frying pan at just the wrong minute, and then he tripped over the pig—"

"The pig?" Mendanbar said. "Where does a pig come into it?"

"It's the family pet. Father says only witches have cats, and he's allergic to dogs. He says that since pigs are intelligent and unusual, they make good pets for enchanters."

"So your father tripped over his pet pig . . ." Cimorene said.

"And the spell went wrong and fixed itself to the frying pan. Both of my parents were furious. Father says that the sort of spell he was using can only ever be cast once by any enchanter, so he's lost his chance at creating the ultimate weapon. And Mother says it was her best frying pan and now she's going to have to start all over breaking in a new one, because you can't cook chicken in the Frying Pan of Doom. It just wouldn't be right."

"I see." Mendanbar blinked. "The Frying Pan of Doom. How . . . unusual. Why did you bring it to us?"

"We didn't know what else to do with it," Tamriff

said. "It's very dangerous—Father says the spell worked perfectly, except for enchanting the wrong object—but he's not quite sure *how* it's dangerous. And we didn't really want to experiment."

"Couldn't you go ahead and give it to a hero?" Daystar asked.

"Father tried. No one would have it. Heroes want a weapon that sounds heroic and magical—the Thunder Mace or the Sword of Stars—not the Frying Pan of Doom. And on top of that . . . Well, here, try to touch it. But be careful."

Gingerly, Daystar reached out and touched the side of the pan. "Ow! It's hot!"

Tamriff nodded. "Nobody can pick it up unless they're wearing an oven mitt. And no hero wants to go into battle wearing an oven mitt and swinging a frying pan—or at least, none of the fifty-seven heroes Father has checked with so far."

"What do you expect us to do with it?" Mendanbar asked.

"Don't you have somewhere you keep dangerous magical weapons?" Tamriff said. "You could put it there."

Mendanbar shook his head. "Things like the Sword . . . er, the Frying Pan of Doom aren't meant to lie about in an armory. It would be asking for trouble."

"Could you and Telemain disenchant the pan?" Cimorene asked.

"That's an idea." Mendanbar studied the frying pan for a moment. "Set it down, Tamriff, and back up a bit. You, too, Daystar." He made some pulling and twisting gestures, and the Frying Pan of Doom began to glow a dull red. Mendanbar frowned and gestured again. The red glow got brighter, and the pan began to make spitting noises, like something being dropped into overheated oil. With a sigh, Mendanbar waved and the glow died. "No, that won't work. I could get the spell off, I think, but I'd use up half of the magic in the Enchanted Forest doing it. We'll have to think of something else."

There was a moment of silence while everyone thought.

"Are you quite sure that *nobody* can pick up that pan without an oven mitt?" Cimorene asked Tamriff at last. "Or is it just that nobody who's tried so far can pick it up?"

"I don't know. Why? Is it important?"

"It might be. Sometimes magic weapons can only be wielded by the proper person, and if so—"

"Then we just have to find the proper person to wield this one," Mendanbar finished. "I think you're right, Cimorene. But how do we do that?"

"The traditional method is to hold a tournament, at which every knight and hero and prince will attempt to use the weapon," Willin said, his tone a curious mixture of interest, disapproval, and dismay. "In this instance, however—"

"Willin, you're a genius," Mendanbar said. "We'll hold a contest. We'll tell people the prize is a powerful magic weapon, but we won't mention what. And we'll get everyone to touch the frying pan, and when the right person does, we'll give it to him."

"How are you going to get all those heroes and knights and princes to touch the frying pan, without telling them what you're doing?" Daystar asked doubtfully.

"We'll make it a contest to prove how well rounded they are," Cimorene said. "They can start with the usual fighting and swordplay and so on, and then we'll have them sing or compose poetry or something, and we'll finish up with a bake-off."

"A bake-off?" Tamriff said blankly.

"A cooking contest. It shouldn't be too hard to arrange for the contestants to touch the frying pan during a cooking contest."

"Heroes and knights won't come to a contest that involves cooking!" Tamriff objected.

"Yes, they will," Mendanbar said. "Willin will arrange it. You have no notion what amazing things Willin can do with large formal occasions. How long will it take to get ready, Willin?"

The little elf puffed out his chest and considered for a moment. "I believe that we can have the invitations out by tomorrow evening, but we ought to allow at least a month before the actual event, to provide everyone with adequate travel time. We can be ready sooner, if you wish, but not as many will attend if we do."

"A month, by all means," the King said. "The more people we have, the better the chance of the right person being there. We'll put the frying pan in the armory in the meantime. As long as it's temporary, I don't think it will be a problem."

"We'll have to hire more kitchen staff," Willin said. He pulled a scroll of paper and a pencil from somewhere in his jacket and began writing. "And at least three more footmen. And we'll need additional prizes for the people who actually win the contests. And—"

"Yes, of course, but first take Tamriff and the pan down to the armory," Cimorene said. "And then see that he gets a decent room. You will be staying until the frying pan has been finally disposed of, won't you?"

Tamriff nodded. "Thank you, Your Majesty."

As Willin and Tamriff started for the door, Daystar frowned at the frying pan. "I'd still like to know what it *does*," he said.

"One thing at a time, Daystar," Cimorene told him.

True to Mendanbar's prediction, an enormous number of heroes and knights signed up for the tournament, despite the unusual requirements. An even bigger crowd arrived to watch the event, and it took a steady stream of footmen and scullery maids to keep the tables by the castle moat supplied with cider and beef patties and ale and fresh gingerbread.

"There is a good deal of speculation as to the nature of the prize," Willin reported as the contestants finished their second round.

"Let them speculate," Cimorene said. "It doesn't hurt anything."

"What if somebody guesses?" Tamriff said in a low, worried tone.

"They won't," Cimorene assured him. "But speaking of the prize, where's the Frying Pan of Doom? It's supposed to be on the big table with the rest of the cooking supplies, but I didn't see it when I went by a minute ago."

Willin turned white. "It's still in the armory. Oh, Your Majesty, I don't know how it happened."

"You forgot," Daystar said. "Never mind. I'll get it." He started for the castle at a dead run.

"Don't forget the oven mitt," Cimorene called after him.

"Why doesn't he just do that popping-out-of-the-air thing?" Tamriff asked. Having been around the palace for a month, he'd had ample opportunity to see Daystar's usual method of getting places in a hurry.

"There are spells to prevent people from using magic too close to the armory," Mendanbar said. "A wizard stole something from me once, and it caused a lot of trouble. Since that business finally got straightened out, I've been more careful." He scowled, as if he was remembering something unpleasant. Then Cimorene touched his arm and he looked at her and smiled.

"The knights are coming," Cimorene said, nodding toward the field. "You'll have to make a speech before they start the bake-off, or Daystar won't be back with the pan in time."

Mendanbar grimaced, nodded, and walked to the front of the tables. The knights and heroes lined up in front of him. Several of them had black eyes from the round of fighting, and one had his left arm in a sling. As Mendanbar began to speak, Cimorene frowned slightly and said in a low voice, "Maybe we should have held the bake-off first. They'd have been in better shape."

"I beg your pardon, Your Majesty, but it wouldn't have worked," Willin said. "Fighting always comes first at a tourney, and they wouldn't have put up with changing the order of events *and* holding a cooking contest."

"I suppose you're right," Cimorene said. "Oh, good, here comes Daystar."

"Where do you want it?" Daystar said.

"On the main table," Cimorene told him. "I'll show you."

Halfway to the table, they were intercepted by a

blond scullery maid in a crisp white apron. "Excuse me, sir," she said to Willin, "but the cook is running out of onions, and he wants to know—"

There was a loud explosion, and an enormous puff of black smoke appeared in the open space behind the tables. Everyone stopped talking and stared, including the knights and heroes. Slowly the smoke cleared, leaving a spreading smell like sour milk and revealing a very tall, thin man wearing a doublet of aquamarine silk, white hose, and a great many diamonds. In a voice that carried to the farthest edges of the crowd, he called, "Annalisa! I know you're here, so you might as well come out. It's time you came home."

"Drat," said the blond scullery maid under her breath, and ducked behind Cimorene. Cimorene looked slightly startled; then she smiled and jerked her head at Daystar. Daystar moved over to stand beside her, effectively screening the scullery maid from sight.

"Annalisa!" the thin man called again.

Mendanbar pushed his crown back on his head and stepped up to the newcomer. "I expect you'll get around to explanations and introductions eventually," he said pointedly.

The thin man tried to look down his nose at Mendanbar, but Mendanbar was too tall for it to work at all well. "I am Rothben the Great, King of the Gracious Islands, and a mighty enchanter."

"He is not!" cried a voice from the crowd of knights, and a handsome, dark-haired man in brightly polished armor pushed his way to the front. "Well, maybe the enchanter part. But Annalisa is the rightful Queen of the Gracious Islands, and I will defend her with my honor and my life. Whether she's here or not."

"Drat *and* bother," said the scullery maid from behind Cimorene and Daystar. "What's Harold doing here?"

"He probably came for the tourney," Cimorene murmured. "Most of them did. You're a princess, I take it?"

"More or less," the scullery maid said.

"I *knew* I should have interviewed all of the new staff myself."

The thin man smiled nastily at Harold the knight. "Ah, Sir Harold. You know, I think you'd be much less nuisance as a pollywog." He pointed, and a long stream of green fire shot from the tip of his finger toward Harold.

Mendanbar made an almost undetectable movement with his fingers, and the green fire vanished before it ever reached the knight. The thin man looked around, startled. "What . . . ? Who did that?"

"I did," Mendanbar said. "I'm the King of the Enchanted Forest, and you can't work magic here without my permission. Particularly not on my guests."

"You are a poor, jumped-up excuse for a king, and I shall teach you a lesson you won't soon forget," said the thin man, and began muttering and gesturing at Mendanbar.

"Oh, dear," said the scullery maid. "Excuse me, Your Majesty, Your Highness, but I have to stop this." Stepping out from her concealment, she called, "Uncle Rothben!"

The thin man stopped gesturing and turned. "Ah, Annalisa. I see you have finally come to your senses."

"Not the way you mean, Uncle," the scullery maid said.

"Say the word and I will spit him where he stands!" Sir Harold said, glaring at the thin man.

"Do be quiet, Harold," said Annalisa. "He'd turn you into a newt or something before you even got close. Uncle, you can't think you're going to get away with kidnapping me in full view of all these people."

"Why not?" said the thin man, walking toward her. "Once we're married—"

"You're my *uncle!* I couldn't marry you, even if you hadn't stolen my kingdom." Annalisa backed away as the enchanter drew nearer, and bumped into Daystar.

"Don't be foolish, girl." The enchanter grabbed her wrist.

"That's quite enough of that," Mendanbar said, and raised his hands. Unfortunately, all the knights and heroes seemed to agree with him. They rushed forward in grand disorder, shouting and getting in each other's way. In the process, one of them managed to knock Mendanbar over from behind. Rothben glanced at the untidy knot of useless people, grinned, and began muttering a spell under his breath.

"Let go of me!" Annalisa pulled away and bumped into Daystar again. Grabbing at his arm for balance, her hand fell on the Frying Pan of Doom. With a cry of satisfaction, she pulled it out of his grasp, turned, and brought it down hard on her uncle's head.

With a noise like a bubble bursting in a pan of boiling water, Rothben the Great turned into an enormous poached egg.

There was a long, startled silence. Then Daystar said in tones of great satisfaction, "So *that's* what the Frying Pan of Doom does."

"The what?" said Annalisa, staring at the poached egg.

"The Frying Pan of Doom," Cimorene said. "It appears that *you* are the proper person to have it. It's not burning your hand, is it?"

"No."

"Good." She signaled Willin to have the castle staff clean up the poached egg, which was oozing messily all over the lawn. "Then we don't have to hold the bake-off after all."

A murmur rose from the crowd. Sir Harold, who had been staring at Annalisa, shook his head and walked over to Cimorene. "Don't cancel the bake-off, Your Majesty. It was officially announced, and it ought to go through." He lowered his voice and added confidentially, "And some of the boys have really been looking forward to it. Not that they'd ever admit it."

So they held the bake-off after all. A barbarian swordsman with gigantic muscles and a fur cloak won with his Quick After-Battle Triple Chocolate Cake, though everyone agreed that Sir Harold's Hack-'N'-Slash Coleslaw had been a strong contender. At least one engagement was broken because the bride-to-be couldn't bear having a fiancé who cooked better than she did, and four others were contracted on the spot by farsighted princesses and ladies who felt that such an arrangement might have distinct advantages in the long run. The barbarian was mobbed by princesses eager to taste his cake and by mothers eager to get hold of his recipe.

"All in all, a very satisfactory conclusion," Mendanbar said, stretching his long legs. The royal family, Willin, Tamriff, Annalisa, and Sir Harold had gathered in the throne room once everyone had gone home, to discuss the events of the day. Annalisa still carried the Frying Pan of Doom, having presented the barbarian swordsman with an enchanted silver ax from the armory and ten pounds of chocolate from the kitchen instead.

"I don't think we're quite done yet," Cimorene said, and looked at Annalisa. "How did you come to be in our kitchen?"

"After my parents died and Uncle Rothben seized the kingdom, my fairy godmother showed up in my bedroom in the middle of the night," Annalisa said. "She told me to leave right away and find a job as a kitchen maid in some other castle."

"Wouldn't it have been better if she offered to help you get your kingdom back?" Daystar said.

"Fairy godmothers tend to be very traditional," Cimorene said. "I doubt that it occurred to her. Was that all, Annalisa?"

"Well, she gave me a dress as shining as the stars and said I was to wear it to the ball. I thought that was a little strange. I mean, I didn't think kitchen maids got invited to balls. I've still got it around somewhere."

"What are you going to do now?" Mendanbar asked.

"She's going back to the Gracious Islands to be queen, of course," Sir Harold said. "And I shall be her faithful knight."

"No, I don't think so, Harold," said Annalisa gently.

"But you have to go back! You're the rightful queen!" Sir Harold looked thoroughly shocked.

"Yes, but I'm going back alone. If I'm going to be a queen, I need to do it myself. If you came, I'd depend on you too much."

Sir Harold looked as if he wasn't sure whether to be flattered or upset. "But what are you going to do about your uncle's cronies and henchmen? He brought in rather a lot of them after you left, you know."

Annalisa looked down at the Frying Pan of Doom and smiled. "Oh, I think I'll be able to handle them somehow."

"I don't know what Father is going to think of this," Tamriff muttered, shaking his head.

"He ought to be pleased," Cimorene said. "His magic creation has found its proper owner, defeated a powerful enchanter, and is about to restore the rightful queen to her throne. What more could he ask?"

"Your father made that?" Sir Harold said to Tamriff, waving at the frying pan.

"Well, he enchanted it. Before that, it was just Mother's best frying pan."

"I've always wanted a magic sword. Do you suppose he would do something a little less dramatic, if I asked very politely?"

Tamriff nodded. "There are plenty of lesser spells he could use."

"Then if Annalisa is sure she doesn't want my help at home—"

Annalisa nodded.

"—I think I'll go with you," Sir Harold said.

"In the morning," Cimorene said firmly. "It's much too late for you to leave now. You'll all be our guests tonight, and you can start off after breakfast tomorrow morning."

Sir Harold started to nod, then caught himself. "As long as you won't be serving poached eggs for breakfast," he said cautiously.

"No poached eggs," Mendanbar said. "And that really *does* take care of everything."

"Not quite," Willin said. Everyone looked at him, and he coughed in mild embarrassment. "We appear to be in need of a new scullery maid."

The visitors looked at each other, Mendanbar chuckled, Daystar shook his head, and Cimorene threw her hands up in the air. "Put an ad in the paper," she said to Willin. "And *this* time, I'm going to interview everyone myself."

"Yes, Your Majesty," Willin said, bowing, and everyone laughed.

Quick After-Battle
Triple Chocolate Cake

Transcribed by Patricia C. Wrede

Transcriber's Note: This is the original recipe as used by the barbarian swordsman. Amounts and instructions for somewhat more conventional kitchens are given in parentheses.

FIRST, ROUND UP THE PRISONERS and have them make a good fire. Pile shields around it to hold in heat. (Preheat oven to 350°.)

Assemble ingredients:

Butter the size of a good spear head (1 stick butter or margarine)

A good big fistful of brown sugar (½ cup brown sugar, packed)

A big fistful of white sugar (½ cup white sugar)

A couple of eggs (2 large eggs)

A good splash of vanilla (2 teaspoons vanilla extract)

Secret Magic Ingredient (2 Tablespoons blackstrap molasses)

Milk from a chocolate cow (⅔ cup chocolate milk)

A small fistful of cocoa (⅓ cup unsweetened cocoa)

Two or three fistfuls of flour (1 cup flour)

Pinch of salt (½ teaspoon salt)

Two pinches soda (1 teaspoon baking soda)

Hunk of chocolate, hacked into bits with second-best sword (1 6-ounce package semisweet chocolate chips)

Pick a small shield and clean it, then grease it up good. Sprinkle in a little flour and save it for later. (Grease and flour a 13" × 9" pan.)

———

In somebody else's helmet, beat butter and brown sugar and white sugar together—make sure helmet is clean before using! Add eggs and beat some more. Add vanilla and Secret Magic Ingredient and beat it all again. (In a large bowl, cream butter or margarine until fluffy. Add brown sugar and white sugar and mix thoroughly. Add eggs, vanilla, and blackstrap molasses, beating well after each addition.)

Stir flour, cocoa, salt, and soda together in whatever is handy. Add to batter, alternating with milk. Beat real good. Stir in chocolate pieces. (In a separate container, stir flour, cocoa, salt, and baking soda together. Beat into butter mixture, alternating with the chocolate milk. Beat for 1–2 minutes, then fold in chocolate chips.)

Dump batter into greased shield. Bake next to fire while gathering loot. Give helmet back to sucker who let you mix cake in it; promise him first piece if he gets too mad. Eat warm while counting loot. Serves two. (Pour batter into greased and floured 13" × 9" pan. Bake 35–40 minutes. Cake should be sort of flat and solid, not light and puffy. Let cool before cutting, or the pieces will fall apart and the gooey chocolate chips will get all over everything. Sprinkle with powdered sugar or top with whipped cream. Serves a lot more than two, even if everybody really likes chocolate.)

Notes from the Author

ONE OF THE THINGS everybody seems to want to ask writers is, "Where do you get your ideas?" When people ask me this, my usual response is, "Ideas are the easy part. The hard part is writing them down." Which is perfectly true—practically every professional writer will tell you that—but doesn't actually answer the question.

So, for the benefit of everyone who really *does* want to know where the ideas come from, here are the stories of how the stories in this book came to be written.

The earliest tale included here is "Earthwitch." I wrote the original story in 1981, and as best I can remember, it began with the image of the terrified invading army sinking slowly into the ground. The original story was my attempt to explain how this had come about. It opened with the king, Evan Ryding-sword, climbing the path to the Earthwitch's cave and ended with the scene on the mountaintop. The story never sold, but it had something in it that wouldn't let go of me. When Jane Yolen asked to see some of my older work for possible inclusion in this collection, it was one of the first stories I thought of.

After reading it, Jane told me she thought it was a possibility, but there were a number of things she felt were not adequately dealt with. To answer her questions, I had to add a second viewpoint, Mariel's, to the story. I also clarified the ending and polished up some of the scenes in the middle.

"Rikiki and the Wizard" was written in 1985 for the second Liavek "shared world" anthology—a collection of short stories by different authors, all of which were set in the same city (or its environs). I had spent a good portion of one morning reading a book of American Indian folktales and had started wondering what sort of folk stories the Liavekans might tell each other, particularly about their not-too-bright chipmunk god, Rikiki. From there, the story practically wrote itself.

The next year, in 1986, I got two letters asking if I would write short stories for anthologies. The first was from Bruce Coville, who rather apologetically in-formed me that he was putting together an anthology of unicorn stories and the deadline was only two weeks away. Did I have any unicorn stories in my files?

I didn't. I checked the "Sorry, no I don't" box on the postcard he had included, put it in the OUT-GOING MAIL basket, and sat down at my computer to work on the book I was supposed to be writing. But I couldn't stop thinking about unicorns. I knew there were unicorns in the Enchanted Forest; in *Talking to Dragons*, which had been published the previous year, I'd mentioned a well where unicorns drank. Naturally, Enchanted Forest unicorns would be beautiful and magical and intelligent—but, being intelligent, they would certainly know just how beautiful and magical they were, and would expect to be treated accordingly. . . . Two hours later, I had written five pages of "The Princess, the Cat, and the Unicorn," and I got up from my computer and tore up the little postcard. By the end of the week, the story was in the mail.

The other request I got in 1986 was from Andre Norton, who was putting together a series of *Tales of the Witch World* anthologies and asked me to contrib-ute. Since the Witch World books were some of my favorites when I was in high school, I couldn't bring myself to say no, but coming up with the story was *work*. I reread all the Witch World books (that part was fun, not work) and decided where and when I wanted to set the story. Then I had to work out who the characters were and what sort of trials they would face, while trying to keep a Witch World "feel" to the story. The result was "The Sword-Seller." Writing it was an extremely conscious and deliberate process, more like the way I often work when I'm writing novels than the way I usually do short stories.

In 1987 I got another request letter. Jane Yolen was editing an anthology of werewolf stories—would I write one? I'd been rereading *The Thousand and One Arabian Nights,* and that background mixed itself up with the idea of werewolves and a somewhat humorous tone and became "The Sixty-two Curses of Caliph Arenschadd." I sent it to Jane.

She turned it down.

Not because it wasn't a good story, she explained, but because the anthology had taken on a darker tone, and a humorous story just wouldn't fit. These things happen; I only pouted for a couple of days. Eventually, I sold the story to Michael Stearns for his anthology *A Wizard's Dozen.*

Later that year I went on an extended trip to Europe. In Germany my then-husband and I drove along the Rhine River, visited Marksburg Castle, and ended up spending an afternoon at the Lorelei cliff. That night, the *Gasthaus* we stayed at was across the street from a bed-and-breakfast place occupied by a busload of energetic high school students on a tour. "The Lorelei" was, obviously, the result. I hardly had to make up anything at all.

In the spring of 1990 a friend and I visited England and Wales and happened to stay in the town of Harlech. The ruins of Harlech Castle, with birds nesting in cracks in the walls, grass growing between the paving stones, and plants trailing undisturbed out of empty windows, caught my imagination. "This," I said to my friend, "is what the Sleeping Beauty castle would have looked like if the prince had never come." And then I went home and wrote about it. The story turned out to be "Stronger Than Time."

The initial idea for "Roses by Moonlight" came from listening to one too many sermons about the parable of the Prodigal Son. I never found that parable altogether satisfactory; it's as if somebody left off the ending. The Prodigal Son comes home, but his elder brother won't come to the welcome-back party. The father goes out to talk to the brother, but the story ends before it says whether the brother went back to the party or not. And then I heard a sermon that dwelt at some length on the elder brother's attitude, and it got me thinking about *his* viewpoint. Or, *hers* . . .

So that's where I started, with Adrian out in the driveway avoiding her sister's party, though the story took its own path very quickly after that. I finished it in 1994.

"Cruel Sisters" is based on a song, or rather, on several different versions of a particular folk song. Child's *The English and Scottish Popular Ballads* lists it as number 10, "The Twa Sisters," and gives two versions. I heard a third version, titled "Cruel Sister," sung by a friend many years ago, and since then I have run across many others. The basic events of the story are always the same. And then, in late 1994, I heard a new version that referred to the king's *three* daughters in the first line. The middle girl disappears after that one line, and we're back to the jealous girl who drowns her sister over a man, but that one mention was enough to make me wonder—what did that middle sister think about all this? So I let her tell her story. I finished it in 1995.

"Utensile Strength" is the only story written specifically for this collection. Jane Yolen asked if I could include another Enchanted Forest story, preferably one that involved some of the characters readers would recognize from my books. I said I'd try. Over lunch with friends a few days later, I was complaining about the vast number of enchanted weapons that appear in fantasy books, comics, and role-playing games. "There are oodles of Lightning Spears and Fire Swords and Broadswords of Ultimate Destruction," I said, "but nobody ever does enchanted *ordinary* things."

"Like what?" asked my friends.

"Oh, like the Frying Pan of Doom," I said, and the minute I said it, I knew that frying pan belonged in the Enchanted Forest somewhere. But what do you *do* with the Frying Pan of Doom? Well, in all the fairy tales, they have to find the person to whom the magic weapon is meant to belong. And it's really only logical that the way to find the proper owner of a magical frying pan is to have a cooking contest. From there, it was all quite straightforward. Well, *relatively* straightforward, as much as anything in the Enchanted Forest is.

Editors usually ask for changes or additions of some sort when an author submits a story, so when I sent "Utensile Strength" to Jane, I was expecting a phone call. I wasn't expecting the particular addition she asked for, though. She wanted the recipe. It was the first time I ever did my "revisions" standing at a mixer instead of sitting at the computer. Two weeks and many chocolate cakes later, I hatched the recipe for Quick After-Battle Triple Chocolate Cake.

So that's where my ideas come from: unexplained pictures in my head, the unexpected intersection of a request for a particular sort of story with whatever I happen to be reading or doing, the logical extension of illogical premises, real things looked at sideways, and even a very conscious and deliberate building up of material. There isn't just one place that ideas come from, and every story is different.

Ideas really *are* all over the place. They're in little towns one stays at by accident on vacation and in songs one hears on the radio, in old folktales and in sermons at church, in casual remarks made by oneself or one's friends. All a writer has to do to get ideas is to really look at and really listen to the things around her.

Ideas are the easy part. The hard part is getting the words down on paper that convey the ideas, and getting the words *right*.

Permissions
Acknowledgments